Booktown Writings

'Time is a river, and books are boats.'
J Fort Newton

Booktown Writings

Published by
Booktown Writers

ISBN 978 0 9930430 0 0

Printed by J & B Print
32a Albert Street
Newton Stewart
DG8 6EJ

layout and design by Mike Clayton
mclayton33@talktalk.net

Cover photograph by Andy Farrington,
Fantastic Eye Photography
www.fantasticeye.co.uk

Contents

Foreword

This collection of stories, the first produced by the Booktown Writers, consists of winning and commended stories from our annual Short Story Competition along with contributions from some of the Booktown Writers own members. It offers a rich and stimulating selection that represents some of the best new short fiction available. From Carol McKay's thought provoking *Flags* (winner in 2012) through to Zoe Gilbert's innovative *Green: How I Love You* (winner in 2013) via tales from Africa, Scotland, North America and the downright fantastical we hope these little boats will take you on an interesting journey.

The Booktown Writers formed in the summer of 2011 in Wigtown, Scotland's National Book Town in beautiful Galloway. We have writers in the group at all stages of development, several with multiple publications of novels, biographies, poetry and short stories. The objectives of the Booktown Writers are to advance, improve and develop regional, national and international literature by:

- ❁ Encouraging regional writers to develop their skills and increase their publications
- ❁ Organising and supporting an annual international short story competition
- ❁ Producing collections of new writing for publication

For more information please go to https://www.booktownwriters.co.uk or visit us at https://www.facebook.com/groups/booktownwriters/ or you can email us at mail@booktownwriters.co.uk

Flags

Carol McKay

She caught a glimpse of herself reflected in a perspex panel at the Tourist Information display while they waited to board the ferry. Slightly dishevelled, her clothes formless now she'd lost weight, she hesitated over which fliers to choose.

She looked, too, at the reflection of her husband. He was lost in his mobile phone, thumbing down through various options, or maybe he was texting someone from work – someone she didn't know or couldn't remember. She pushed her glasses up her nose, more from habit than from the need to see sharply.

Once on board, Scott pointed to the plush seating. 'Grab a window seat. I'll get the sandwiches.'

It was lovely to be at sea again. How long had it been? She would ask him when he came over. Whole panels of light glossed on the water as the sun reflected on it out of a patch of blue. Sunlight was brighter, here, at the coast, yet the water itself was black-blue, undulating like one of those cats – what were they called? – rippling its skin to relieve an itch. And when she strained to see behind her, there was the wide white wash spilling and levelling out behind them.

'We're underway,' she told him when he returned with the sandwiches.

'Let the holiday commence!' He set down his own food on the tray hinged to the chair in front and peeled open her sandwich pack.

'I can do that,' she protested.

He held out the first sandwich, wrapped in a napkin; held it there till she met his eyes then he said, 'Let's enjoy every moment.'

She nodded, forced her face to mirror his smile then they settled to enjoy the crossing.

Three days they would spend in the Republic, tracing their family tree, and three days in the North. Or Ulster. She couldn't remember the politically correct terms for them. They seemed like completely different countries because of the different money, different systems of measurement, different road signs and different colours of bunting criss-crossing the streets.

That was the biggest shock when they disembarked from the ferry: all the flag waving. A sign of a people who felt their identity was at risk, Scott said: people who felt in danger of being overwhelmed. Union Jacks and the red hand of Ulster waved at the tops of lampposts all along the road. As if people were likely to forget who they were or where they came from.

She listened to him without much focus but two of his phrases penetrated. She thought about them for what she hoped would be long enough to make them stick.

The drive to Sligo was a good one. He drove and she looked out of the window. Some things were similar. They had a problem, here, with overgrowing Buddleia self-seeding everywhere, just like in Glasgow. Ragwort, too, in great bouquet clumps of yellow, burst out of every bit of wasteland beside the road. 'Invasive species, just like at home,' she said to him, pointing, and he took his eyes off the road briefly without responding.

Invasive species. No respecters of political boundaries. Maybe that's what their ancestors had been, settling in Scotland and infiltrating the gene pool. She pulled down the sun visor and looked at herself in its mirror. She didn't look Irish because Irish were blond haired like the butcher in the local shop when she was growing up. Or maybe they were really dark, like Dana had been, or that musical Corr family. Was that stereotyping? She glanced again at her husband. Ginger-blond hairs thatched the backs of his hands on the steering wheel and the skin on his forearms was barely protected by their sparse reddish veil. He was so different from her with her hair still deep brown, with no help from a hairstylist's bottle. Yet they both came from the Irish, in part at least.

It was wet when they reached Sligo and all the shops had closed. They wandered round the town that evening, slightly adrift, imagining in which spartan room her grandmother might have been born a century ago, the turbulent Garavogue river coursing under the Hyde Bridge then as now like a pounding bloodline. Over the next few days, she took photos and videos, turning 360 degrees to capture it all so this connection with her family's place she'd rediscovered wouldn't ever be lost.

The day they left was still and clear with the Garavogue river, heading out to sea, widening out, liquid blue-green. It was the kind of day and weather for dallying and they had plenty of time to drive to their hotel in the east. North. The car climbed up the road heading for Enniskillen through a tunnel of leafy trees, up the sweeping hillsides. To their right, above the treeline, the hills became mountainous; craggy: a bulbous rocky top and a sheer sweep like the silky green A-line dress she'd worn at her wedding. How many years ago? To their left, below the trees, the ground dropped to a valley before rising up again on the other side, the whole world drenched in green.

'Let's go and explore,' Scott said, turning sharp left at a sign for a lake and waterfall. He steered the car down the steep pathway a thousand feet, perhaps, in a space of moments, till they were scooped up in a cup of green. Even the lake was green, sometimes rippled by a faint wind, sometimes silvered with light and mirror smooth. He cranked on the hand brake and wound down the window for her, using the control switch on the driver's door. Then he switched off the engine. That slight breeze stirred them through the open window, teasing her hair. After a moment, they got out. A plaque informed them the two round discs they could see on the lake were crannogs that had been inhabited a millennium ago but were now just small flat 'islands' with one or two scrubby bushes on them.

Strange to think that life had gone on here and had ended. History submerged, as it were, and vanished without much trace. The only life forms now, other than half a dozen visitors, were sheep in the grassy field between the car park and the water and crows flapping into and out of a tree, cawing.

'Quite a place to live,' he said, and took a photograph. 'Not taking any snaps?'

11

She reached for her camera. 'Oh – out of memory, it says.' Only half way through their holiday, too. 'It must have been all those videos.'

'Too bad.' He focused his lens on her and clicked. 'We'll upload them when we get to the hotel and you can start again.'

That was a nice idea. Upload your memories and start again.

He bought her a tub of ice-cream then told her to stay where she was, leaning against the fence, while he went to the toilet. 'It's over there,' he said, pulling lightly on her shoulder to point it out. 'Just behind you.'

She nodded, spooning ice-cream into her mouth.

'Don't move.'

'Stop worrying!' She smiled fully into his eyes to reassure him.

Out of memory. She set down the empty tub on the fence post and thought of her camera. She took out the memory card and looked at it, amazed that all those photos and videos of where her ancestors had lived could be held on that little flat rectangle of plastic.

A swallow flicked past, flying low over the field and she reached for her binoculars to follow it. The remains of the crannog filled the lens and she wondered again about the way of life and the people who'd lived there. Possibly ancestors. Vanished without much trace.

'Ready?'

Scott was behind her, waiting for her, and she gathered up all her things in a fluster and settled herself back into the car. The rest of the drive was easy; the road signs were British and familiar. It felt like home with a slightly different accent. They pulled up outside the country house hotel and stepped into a world of thick red upholstery and beeswaxed wood, dined on roast beef with gravy then returned to their room to stretch out on their damask-covered bed.

Later, Scott took her camera to upload her photos but when he flipped open the compartment it was empty. 'Where's the card?' he asked, and stared at her.

What had she done with it? She felt the water inundate her, filling up her chest. She squeezed her hands in tight to shore herself up against it and shook her head. 'I don't remember.' She saw his mouth press down at the corners.

He moved the laptop off his knee and set it beside him on the bed then reached for her hands, separated one and held it. 'Think about it. What did you do with it?'

She pulled her hand back to keep it for herself, not linking to him, but he held on to it as if he had a right; as if the contact might help the memory surface. 'Let go of me and I'll find it.'

She turned out her bag. Unzipped and rezipped all the sections. Took out her compact mirror and her eye shadows, her lipsticks and plastic wallet of make-up brushes, her comb and lip-gloss but it wasn't there. Scott lifted her diary from the bed and riffled through the pages but only a desiccated three-leafed clover fell out. She checked her pockets. She checked everywhere. One silly rectangle of plastic and all her photographs were lost with it. 'Stupid!' she said, scolding herself. 'I'll never remember it now.' And that was the nub of it.

He put his arms round her and kissed her hair over her ear so loudly it hurt. 'We've got the rest of the holiday. Remember I said? "Let's enjoy every moment." And not worry about anything else.'

It was another thing lost but what could she do? At least he'd taken some shots with his but it wasn't the same. Scott called room service and ordered a bottle of wine. That took the edge off it and then they lay together with their limbs entangled, her mouth on the smooth skin of his shoulder, till she fell asleep.

Next day, they headed north to the coast. The weather had turned wild, grey and blustery, yet there was no rain. She sat in the passenger seat with the road map open across her knee while he drove round the twisting scenic route. Stopped for a moment, they left the car and clambered on white rocks that were sharp, yet crumbling like huge sticks of the pipe clay her mother used to clean the tenement stairs with. Funny she should remember that.

They took a walk down to the beach over dunes and yellow sand, the wind whipping her hair around her like snakes around Medusa only she felt it was she who was calcifying, her thoughts all turning to stone.

Further east and high up, they pulled into a lay-by to try to gauge their bearings. Matching angles where road and map met, she exulted in recognising the smoky double land masses of the Isle of Islay on the horizon, with Kintyre on the right. That Scotland and Ireland were so close as to be visible! It surprised her. The kingdom of Dalriada was over there, settled by Irish people who knew themselves as Scots and gave that name to a nation. Her nation.

They ate lunch in the car, plums and cheese sticks and bread spread with little portions of butter sneaked from the hotel at breakfast-time. Scott reached into his back-pack and passed her pill without speaking, and the bottle of water, and she filled her mouth with gulp after gulp of it, thinking of the memory card and praying the pill would put an end to this erosion of her memory or at very least slow it. Then they drove on, a further bend revealing the island of Rathlin, brittle white chalk cliffed.

At length, under continuing grey sky, they left the main road and turned along a quieter stretch uphill towards the causeway. They parked in a railway car park. A shrill whistle sounded and, as they watched, an engine not much bigger than their car sent up a spume of white steam before dragging its train of coaches from the station. 'Like stepping back in time,' Scott said just before he got out of the car. Then, 'It's windy,' he said, bending his head through the open door to her. 'Don't forget your jacket.'

They walked hand in hand to the crossroads and from there, past a squat complex of gift shops and hotel buildings, past a building site whose placards, shuddering in each squally blast, announced that next year, a brand new improved facility would be ready for visitors. He gripped her hand and she wondered, then, if he worried about what next year might bring them, too.

There were crowds around them. So many people had come from such disparate parts of the globe. Japanese people, Dutch, North American, Irish and English – she heard a Babel of languages yet saw the same facial expressions. The gale caught them as they reached the turn in the path. She looked out at the land and seascape in front of them. The sky and sea were bruised and vast. At a distance, white crescents lifted and fell on the water. To the right, ahead of them, the land rose, stark and craggy: blue-grey headlands punctuated by sudden drops, sharp and jagged plummets. The path led down towards the water's edge. She stopped, clinging to the railing and bracing herself against the wind that pounded at her back, her feet unsure on the loose, sandy surface.

'Careful!' he warned.

Her anger cracked. 'I'm not a baby!'

Four young American women overtook them, chatting and laughing and stopping every few yards to take photographs. 'I used to be like that,' she called to Scott. 'Good at things.' Ordinary things like walking downhill on a slippy path. Taking photographs. She used to be good at a lot of things.

More people passed. The wind blew her hood up and when she shoved it down she saw a man, staring at her. Mostly bald but with fine ginger tufts that flipped in the wind he stood staring at her, just staring, and for a moment –

'Give me your hand,' he said and grasped on to her, anchoring her by tucking her hand under his arm so she could walk holding on to him and the railing. And for a moment, she thought the wind must be making his eyes water, too, then he was talking again and saying, 'That's better, eh?' and squeezing her arm tucked in under his.

When they reached the bottom, the rocks spread out in great slabs and flagstone steps to the sea. It was less windy, here; boys scrambled over the rock columns to reach the plateau on the top from where they waved for photographs. She reached into her bag and brought out her camera.

'What are you doing?' he asked, his voice faint against the wind.

'I want to take a photograph,' she said, slipping the strap over her wrist and pressing the 'on' switch.

'But you haven't got the memory card.' His voice faded then came back. 'Remember?'

She stared at him, puzzling over his frown then glanced at the screen. 'It says "5". I've five to take. Or I've taken five.'

'Show me?'

And there were five old photos from the day she'd got the camera: photos of a day she'd forgotten had ever happened. They were saved in the camera's own limited memory.

He was grinning, squeezed in close to look at them. 'It's from when we went to Mull,' he said. 'Remember the trip to Staffa?'

Fingal's Cave on Staffa! Those same hexagonal columns, that same dark grey basalt. She remembered the waves showering up and disintegrating against the rocks, just like today, and those neatly fitting flags under her feet. And that was in Scotland, just across the waves, beyond the clouded horizon. The steps were there from one to the other. She couldn't see it; she'd forgotten all about it. It didn't mean the connection didn't exist.

'You told me they were afraid of being overwhelmed; of losing their identity,' she said, tucking her fingers out of the cold into his warm hands inside his jacket pockets. 'When we saw the flags just after we came off the ferry. Remember?'

He nodded.

She smiled a little, watching people in their bright red and pink anoraks climb up the pillars to reach the top – posing for photographs, staking their claim, flagging up 'I did this'. Distance and perspective made them tiny.

Poor Scott. He was the one who was going to be left, remembering. Let's enjoy every moment, he'd said to her. That meant this rock-face, these wide blue nodding harebells, these tight cupped purple bells of heather – even those invasive species – the wind tossing her and him as they stood together, and the crush of other people, with the sea swollen in front of them.

Carol McKay writes fiction, poetry and life writing, and teaches creative writing through The Open University. In 2010 she won the Robert Louis Stevenson Fellowship, and in 2012 she was delighted when her story *Flags* won the inaugural Booktown Writers' Short Story Competition. Her fiction has appeared in *Gutter, Southlight, Chapman, Mslexia* and other magazines, and was published by PotHole Press as the ebook *Ordinary Domestic: collected short stories*. Her poems have featured in *The Istanbul Review 4* and *Gutter 10*. She reviews fiction for leading UK book organisation Booktrust as well as contributing to their Translated Fiction blog, and she reviews for the litmag *Northwords Now*. Her website is http://carolmckay.co.uk

Encounters with Marcia

Sue Hoffman

The last time I saw Marcia she was on the 127 bus from Sedgefield to Fellerton. It was late on a Tuesday evening. She was sitting alone on the back seat, in the corner, her face pressed to the grimy window, incongruous in pearls and that low-cut cocktail dress she'd worn to Amanda and Jeff's anniversary do.

You don't always notice people at first, do you? I mean you don't go staring at everyone on a bus to see if it's someone you know. It's quite easy to find you've travelled the whole way right across the aisle from, say, your next-door neighbour and only realise it when you both get off at the same stop. Not with Marcia, though. One quick glance was enough to be sure that it was her, and I couldn't pretend otherwise.

I sat down a couple of seats in front of her and tried my very best not to turn round. Unfortunately, that familiar, prickling sensation that trickles up and down my spine whenever she's around just wouldn't go away so, in the end, turn round I did. She was looking straight at me.

There were only three other people on the bus – a young bloke and his girlfriend, busy in an amorous embrace, and a large, hefty man lighting up under the "No Smoking" sign – and I didn't think they'd appreciate being interrupted by my telling them about Marcia. They wouldn't have taken any notice of me in any case.

I was still about half a mile from home and it was raining quite heavily but the rain doesn't bother me so I got off at the next stop. I wondered if she'd follow me but she stayed on the bus, face against the window, watching me standing there. She didn't wave or anything as the bus drove off; she just stared at me.

It had all begun straight after the funeral and, as you can well imagine,

17

it was something of a shock the first time it happened. I didn't want to go to the funeral in any case, but circumstances dictated the necessity. Well, there I was outside the church, thinking about Marcia, and there she was, right next to me on the pavement.

I didn't linger.

The second time I saw Marcia was at night – well, in the early hours of the morning, to be precise – and it proved in a peculiar way to be both more expected and more frightening at the same time. If you're going to see ghosts, it somehow seems normal (if that's the right expression for such an experience) to come across one in the darkness rather than in broad daylight like that first meeting. Seeing someone in your bedroom, someone you know has departed this world, is unnerving enough to say the least, but to have that figure calmly sit on the edge of the bed and to actually feel a slight downward shift of the mattress is guaranteed to ruin a night's sleep.

The mind is surprisingly resilient, though, and it's possible to convince oneself that the nasty experience of a ghost in the bedroom was just a nightmare.

It wasn't so simple to dismiss it the third time. After all, having a necklace fastened for you when there's no one else around is pretty much guaranteed to persuade you that all is not as it should be.

I suppose a bit of our social history might help here, so I'll fill in a few details.

We'd been friends since junior school, Marcia and I. Not all the time, and not inseparable or anything like that, but close enough that it came as both a nasty surprise and a crushing disappointment when Marcia stole Tony from me. I think what upset me most was that she went ahead even though she knew he'd proposed to me.

"You should have said yes straight away if you wanted him," she told me when I sought consolation from her after he'd admitted he was seeing someone else. "Men like Tony don't come around all that often and you have to grab your chance."

I thought she was being sympathetic, until I learned who that "someone" was.

I blamed Tony at first, but I've since come to believe he never stood a chance once Marcia set her green-eyed gaze upon him. In retrospect, she'd undoubtedly wanted him from the time she and I met him, and the fact that he chose me and not her must have irritated worse than a mosquito bite between the shoulder blades. At any rate, I'm quite certain he wouldn't have left me for her had it not been for the lies she told about me.

Devious is far too mild a word to describe Marcia Kellerman. She didn't say anything directly to Tony, of course. No, instead she "confided" to Amanda that she'd seen me out on three different occasions with Gregory Pike from the Accounts Department at work. She wouldn't have mentioned it, she'd told Amanda, because they could have been quite innocent meetings to do with work – except that she'd seen us kissing and it wasn't, in her humble opinion, a platonic kiss between mere colleagues.

Naturally, Amanda reported all this to Jeff who passed it on to Tony and it was this that started to sour our relationship. To say it was galling would be a veritable understatement; I don't even like Gregory Pike. Anyhow, dear Marcia was there to offer solace to poor Tony, and I'll bet she fabricated more stories about me while worming her way into his affections.

I learned all this later, of course. All I knew at the time was that Tony started to change in his attitude toward me. He became more distant and certainly more secretive. Gradually it dawned upon me that he was being unfaithful, but back then I didn't know it was with Marcia. Anyway, Tony and I had a blazing row and I told him to leave.

It was at Amanda and Jeff's anniversary party that I finally found out just how Marcia had manipulated things. Amanda and Jeff had been married for ten years, and of course they invited both me and Tony because Tony had been Jeff's best man and I'd been Amanda's bridesmaid. I did have a few qualms about being at the same venue as Tony after our recent and somewhat acrimonious parting but I decided we should behave in an adult manner and at least be civil to each other.

Sometime during the evening, Amanda took me to one side and said how pleased she was that Tony and I seemed to be getting on well together again and how sorry she was that she'd felt compelled to tell

Jeff what Marcia had said about me and Gregory. Well, I pretended I knew what she was on about and thus managed to discover just what my so-called friend Marcia had been up to.

I've never been one to hide my feelings and the argument Marcia and I had could probably have been heard several streets away. Who cares if it ruined Amanda's little get-together? She shouldn't have indulged in unsubstantiated gossip in the first place.

I recall quite clearly giving Tony a whacking slap across the face, and I would have done the same to Marcia if she hadn't been so cowardly as to leave before I could clobber her too. She drove off pretty speedily – but my car is faster than hers.

Needless to say, the police held an investigation. They were never able to prove that it was anything other than an accident, though, and maybe that was the trouble. If "unlawful killing" or "causing death by dangerous driving" had been the verdict, perhaps justice would have been served and Marcia would not have become such a troubled soul.

So, that's probably all you need to know as background. What I suppose I should admit now is that in a perverse sort of way I've come to enjoy my encounters with Marcia. Doors open unexpectedly. A hairbrush moves across the dressing table. Steaming soup turns stone cold as soon as it is placed on the table. Each of these is thrilling in its own fashion. However, none of them quite compares to actually seeing someone else gazing back at you instead of your own reflection, though, does it? Imagine the scene if you can: you're all dressed up in your finery, the outfit you wore to that fateful anniversary party in point of fact; you do a quick check in the mirror – and what do you see? The face of someone you thought you'd disposed of successfully.

If I'm truthful, it was after the mirror incident that I realised I've become a bit of a junkie as far as these ghostly appearances were concerned. Without conscious volition, I find myself thinking of Marcia, and there she'll be. Never in my life have I felt anything like the adrenaline rush I've been getting whenever I find her nearby.

At present, I'm sitting here at Marcia's desk, using her paper and her favourite pen and wondering if she'll turn up at any moment. I do hope so. It's about time I tried to talk to her, don't you think? Meanwhile,

I've been writing all this down even though I don't know if Marcia, or anyone else for that matter, will be able to read it. The words are clear enough to me, but who knows how much those on the other side can see? I'd like Marcia to read it; I really would.

Nowadays, each time I see her she seems ever more weary, confused, careworn and quite delightfully terrified. Mind you it's only to be expected that sanity begins to go out of the door when you have a deceased person as your almost constant companion, isn't it? It's certainly what's happening to Marcia and I don't feel the slightest twinge of remorse. I think she deserves everything that's coming to her. Not only did she steal Tony from me but she deliberately drove her car straight into mine.

As I mentioned earlier, when I last saw Marcia she was on the bus. That won't be the final time we meet, though. I'm having far too much fun haunting her.

For as long as Sue Hoffman can remember, she has enjoyed writing stories, poems and articles. During her teaching career she wrote scripts for school plays, poems for assemblies and various projects for her classes. She took a year out from teaching to study for an M.A. in Language Teaching and Learning. Now retired, she still tries to write as often as possible, although the dog, budgies and hamster take up much of her time!

Sue has had several short stories shortlisted or placed in competitions, with two winning entries, and thirteen stories have been published in anthologies, magazines or online.

In May 2013, her first novel – a fantasy story entitled *High King* – was published by Circaidy Gregory Press.

Green, How I love You

Zoe Gilbert

Inspired by
"Verde, que te quiero verde"
(Federico Garcia Lorca, *Romance Sonambulo*)

The cold was sharp as light that day, casting chills in place of shadows in the brown, branching wood. There was no wind, but Carlos traced flurries in dead leaves and thought of mice, a furry undercurrent in the fungus-spotted mulch. His beard prickled, his toes ached in his hardening boots, and the numbing peace he sought was starting to seep, familiar, when the song wisped through his head.

Green, how I love you, Green, it sang. It was neither his voice, nor his thought.

Green skin, green hair, oh how I love you, Green. Carlos circled a bare beech tree and tried to smirk. There's no green to be seen anywhere, and what is this? He shook his head, to shake out the voice, and let the cold sink back in. There is succour in cold, one pain replacing another.

He trudged in the still brown air, stale for want of a tree's breath, towards a place where the brambles churned and a slight slope made for a view. Not green but grim, he thought. Grim was his goal in these deadening walks and he knew how to become as numb as a stump, rigid right through, to forget for a time what was lost.

He made for the dint in a long-fallen trunk, his favoured seat, and in the final strides of his approach there seemed to unfurl, right there in the bark's old crease, a fungus. He stopped, and bent over it. Had he not noticed it, his steps automatic, his eyes tired? A velvet brown ear glistened, so new, so soft, it looked warm.

There was a scurrying away beyond the trunk, a quivering through the brambles. Carlos bent closer, caught a scent of something like truffle, like chestnuts sweetly charred, and he whispered into the ear.

Green, how I love you.

22

He started back. In the windless wood, impossible leaves long flown from the trees whispered in return so that he seemed caught amidst a chorus. Green skin, green hair. Carlos stumbled further up the slope, stamping down curls of thorn, shaking his head again to chill his cheeks and sluice himself back to his senses.

The hill crested soon, he knew, and would show him a bank of sky, but the trees reared up with the heaving ground, confusing his path, and their bodies were rich with dark ringlet moss. His palms as he grasped were stroked by it. As his hands slid down it licked at his wrists and he was maddened by the thrum he felt in response.

There is no green, he said in his head. No green, no love, now breathe in this cold and take it down and hold it. Cold is comfort now.

He bent over, breathing, so far down that he saw the wood between his legs. But the warmth of his breath made him furious, the heat of his folded belly and his hot hands on his knees and he let out a groan backwards down the slope. His head hurt and his ears began to ring. The familiar beat of blood, he thought, at least that is how it should be, but the ringing was tinged with a high-strung note that was not red but green, the fine green of grass tips, of saplings, sap, the green blood of trees.

He saw her then, the singing thing. Or he saw through his legs a waver like heat in the air, and the dead leaves rising in it. Green, how I love you. It rang in his ears, and the hum of it purled through his veins and then she was gone. The wood faded back to sepia but for a tint, the hint of sap that glowed now from deep within each tree.

Carlos righted himself and turned and ran down the slope. He felt the last threads of her wavering heat in the air and his mouth watered at the scent of chestnut, of smoke.

He followed it like a bloodhound, but as he crouched down, nose to the ground, the shiver ahead would slide up and shake old man's beard in a taunting cloud or leave tumbling specks of lichen. Then up he would gaze, running hands-out, with the chaos of canopy crazing his eyes only to hear her whisk through the leaf litter, marking his path up ahead with heel dints that he probed with muddy fingers.

How far he went or for how long, no tree in the wood or thought in his head made measure, and what did it matter? For he found the place – her place – and how perfect, how secret it was.

The song curled through his mind but Carlos did not know how to sing. He was all breath, after the chase, and he smelled his own sweat and the blood in his pulse disgusted him. The shirt that clung to his sticky flesh, the wool that protected his beating skin, he threw off, and he rubbed himself with leaves. They were dry, paper brown, and he shuddered at their lifelessness but breathed in deep all the same.

He knew what to do. Naked, speckled with leaf fragment, he crawled between leaning slender lengths of birch and beech. They made a tunnel that funnelled him down into a gully, where the musk overwhelmed him and the ground grew soft with mulch. Every chestnut breath was a draught to his veins; every close of his eyes brought her nearer, and when he thought he murmured her song it was her voice that thrilled him.

Green, how I love you, Green. Carlos rolled in the bed of leaves strewn in the gully's depth, green and red and rustling brown, and when she finally crept upon him, he sang too.

It was not like birds, like the cries of love, or like a ballad that worships the woods. He became a chord that would play with no tune but her, and had no resonance except for her response. Green skin, green hair, his limbs seemed to say, and those were the only words he wanted now, all he would ever want.

He learned more quickly than ever he had, as if woodland ways are given. How to bury into the ground and borrow the soily sleep of earthworms; how to follow mud to water and lap with his tongue. But best of all, how to tap the sap that rose all around him, the sign of it in the air growing so clear that it pierced his head and made an orchestra of it with its sweet high notes and throbbing drone, whether at leaf or root. Green's own hard tongue, made so much stronger than his own by life, would turn for hours against a wrinkle of birch bark, until the juice found course and poured down her chin. Then she fed him, and he bit at her lips, so hard to feel between his own that had barely lived at all.

It hurt him at first, the sense of what had been wasted, his mind cramped all these years by thoughts that came in such limited shapes, hardening out the wild world beyond. Whatever he had left, whatever had been lost, shrank to a small red stone, hard and silent. Then, in his bliss, he forgot even this.

Carlos grew slender and so his limbs seemed to lengthen, their pale angles dotted with leaf shred, so that he felt a kinship with the silver birches that lent stripes of moonlight to the wood at night, and that yielded so gracefully to Green's sweet, hard tongue. So attuned did he become to Green, the colour of her song and her mischievous quiver, that her form became more and more distinct to him. In bright beetle backs he discovered her eyes; in the old pollards he traced the sharp line of her shoulders, until sometimes he glimpsed the whole of her as she swept through a clearing, or wound her way up the trunk of an oak to send down showers of acorns.

Without speech, without time, it was no surprise now to watch a trumpet of fungus bloom from a stump, and always before he teased it away with tender fingers, he would sing first to its sensuous ear, Green, how I love you, Green, and he knew she would hear.

Their gully, under its stripling roof, grew musty with Carlos's scents, the pungency of his shrinking flesh a note that soured her aura of truffle and chestnut. When the wood began to change, dressing itself with a shy, verdant growth, he scattered these tiny dapple-leaves into fresh beds for them, and rubbed himself raw with what was left. Still, the freshly excited air vibrated, and foxes came, drawn through the warming, prickling wood. He felt the damp nose of a vixen dotting his thighs one night, and she carried away the smell of him like a secret while Green pulsed against his side, invisible in her veil of sap. He felt himself betrayed and betrayer, and was shocked to find these words in his head.

With the spring came other disturbing sounds that froze Carlos still in his leaf-litter bed. One was a crunch, that brought back to his mind that small red stone. The next was a sting, a call that was not a bird but had the same joyous thrall about it, and made pain weave through his head. The air was shot with sun in that moment, and heat on his skin made him shudder for something, a feeling he could not grasp. Green trailed away like smoke through the undergrowth and his hard white limbs could not follow.

25

Far up from the gully the earth shook. Trees tensed their roots, and Carlos tensed too. Green, where are you, Green? he gasped, and it was no song at all, but a terrible wheeze that tore at his unused throat. The tumult of tones grew too much to bear, and his thoughts made another word: voices. But the word was so strange that he let it dissolve in his mouth. Bury, he thought in its place; burrow down, and he wriggled his elbows, his wasted hips, and felt the leaves scrape the dirt from his withered skin.

Plump pink hands dragged at his roof, tearing away rich shadow. Shrieks as foreign as parrots burst above Carlos.

"This is the place! Let's make a castle, with dungeons!" The voices cut shapes in his head then, hard and angled and irresistible. Carlos groaned with new remembered pain, the spikes of words pricking him so that he longed to roll instead in coils of brambles, have his sap speared from him but not blood, not red.

Green, he wheezed, but the sound, love cramped into a mere word, was all that was left.

A pink face peered, small and round. Carlos turned away, pressed leaves into the creases of his own numbed cheeks.

"Go back to the car, right now," said the words. "God, the smell. What the hell do we do?"

He heard someone start to cry. Only human beings cry, he thought, only flesh and blood. Is it me? Is it me, crying?

"Can't we call someone? Do they even have wardens out here? God, I can't breathe, it's foul. I don't care if he can hear me. Did the kids see? Give me the phone, we should call the police. Don't touch him. I said don't touch him."

Carlos searched in his limbs for the sense of tightening tree roots, the swallow of silent birds, and it was all gone. There was only a faint thud, thud, thud, that came from his red human heart.

Zoe Gilbert lives in London but writes stories that take place anywhere but cities; these are most often inspired by real folklore and folk tales. She draws most of her inspiration from Scottish folklore, and is writing a short story collection using these ideas for her PhD in creative writing. Zoe has had flash and short fiction published in various UK/Irish anthologies, and journals such as *Luna Station Quarterly, Fringe Magazine, Glint,* the *British Fantasy Society Journal* and *Vineleaves.*

Cutting the Roses

Jane Archer

Rose Williams has a sweetness all of her own. She understands a world closed in by the ones She loves; she understands me. We discuss things of an intimate nature. It makes Rose blush and turn away. Her mother, Miss Edwina, didn't believe in sex. Rose told me in hushed tones that God-fearing Miss Edwina recognised the necessity of procreation and that it was simply a matter of endurance. She did not like the idea of bodies sharing wetness and salt and skin and rhythm while God watched on. Rose said that it was stricter in those times and she could be right.

The other day I looked at Rose's fragile, fluttering eyes and the soft copper curls nudging her narrow shoulders. I wanted to pull her to me, but I didn't. Jiggs, the pudgy-faced Boston terrier, occupied her lap. It hadn't been a good day as there had been much raving about her grandfather the impostor.

'An impostor?' I said. 'Either he's your grandfather or he's not.'

She gave me that all knowing, perfectly paranoid look, and shrugged. Eyeing my old dressing gown and woolly Penguin slippers, she said: 'just dreadful, you need to think of changing your clothes or you'll never find a beau.'

Watching her flip the dog's ears up and down, I said, 'you seem a little mad today, Rose.'

'You must never make fun of insanity, dearest; it is the most tr-aa-gic of things.' She looked up. 'My mother was in the bin, you know?'

I hadn't known that the woman who signed her own daughter over to the state asylum had been sectioned herself.

Rose became animated: arms stretched out and hands drew circles in the air. 'Yeees. Poor Miss Edwina, she had to call my brother in the middle of his sojourn to ask him to come and rescue her. They said she was a hysteric. Superficial and artificial. Can you believe it?'

The squashed face of the dog let out a quick yip as though in agreement.

I liked listening to Rose and letting the words spread out in front of me with that drawling Southern accent. The sound brought humid heat and the stickiness of swamps. I knew I loved this girl who left a pitcher of iced water outside her bedroom door, who had an addiction to root-beer, who adored dresses and knew what was tacky and what was true. She bounced Jiggs on her knee as though he were a baby; but I was tired. I took a big blue tablet, the one that prods my tonsils on the way down, and sleep finally came.

When I went to the last meeting it was a Tuesday in April and spring had made its bright announcement with daffodils and bells of blossom. Old winter sun had given birth to a young cheeky thing that pushed fingers of light through the bruised windows of the train. There was something inside the carriage: the rhythm, the electric heartbeat. It reminded me of being alive. The line of the coast moved along, keeping up and being left behind. I could have been on a day-trip to one of the villages with their ragged shores and soft-sand beaches, laid out for families used to rain and gritty sandwiches; but I was on my way to Dundee.

I liked Dundee.

Dundee was reassuring. The place was no stranger to the messy business of letting the mad in and keeping them there. It had a history of the lunatic asylum, 'The Liff', nearby. I was in the safe hands of a city that cared for me, that treated me, that gave me a chance.

When I arrived Dr Barney was ready as usual. In the beginning I had hoped for a name with more muscle, more clout. One of Rose's doctors was called Dr Freeman. He sounded like a pioneer or a liberator of slaves, whereas Barney was a school teacher or cartoon character. But Dr Barney's warmth worked. He went through my notes again: what else can we try, Roseanne? What else can we do? He spoke in short, lilting sentences. I could no longer press a finger to my nose or slip my foot in a shoe without loathing or exhaustion, and he saw this. He knew

I sank deep; words could barely form; he saw the ripple of the next breath, which surprised me when it came. He saw me. Finally, with one eyebrow lifted into the question, he asked whether it had to be done. This was when I told him yes, again, yes. There is no other way.

By the time I got home the evening had already taken on a sadness of its own and a dark bluish air hung in the room. Little was said between Rose and me. Usually, Rose loved to chat, to tell stories, to give glory to glamour. But there was no mention of the fittings at Saks or outings to the opera and tea dances. She held a silk hanky in her hand and rubbed it against her fingers. I counted her steps as she paced backwards and forwards. Dainty feet barely touched the carpet while I memorised the numbers. I have kept everything I have ever read about Rose, yet the story still shocked me when it came.

She told me that in 1943, when she was in her early thirties, a doctor cut her brain even though he wasn't sure what he was doing. He gave Rose a mild form of anaesthesia and drilled two small holes in her temple, to the side of each eye. Rose saw what appeared to be a butter knife going in and something like a carpenter's mallet tap, tap, tapping the handle. The knife was swung around as the doctor asked Rose to sing God Bless America.

> God Bless the Land that gave us birth!
> No pray'r but this know we
> God bless the land, of all the earth,
> The happy and the free…

And then recite the Lord's Prayer. When she could no longer talk, he stopped. After the procedure she was put in a sanitorium called 'Institute for the Living' as she could no longer look after herself. I did not move to comfort her. Instead I watched her weep, grieving for a lost life, even though she did not die until 1996. Slowly her sobs subsided as a sound of soft tapping lulled me to sleep.

The day before my admission to hospital Rose sat in a corner of the living room as I slunk around the house, keeping close to the walls. The dog's chin was flat on Rose's knee. I had cleaned the bathroom for the second time that day and the eighth time that week, if you include the quick wipe down before bed yesterday. The germs must regret taking up residence in my bathroom. In other homes they would have had a long and fruitful life. Making yourself invisible doesn't work against someone or something devoted to destroying you.

I peered out the living room window. A big greedy sky hung around the tenement block, eating away at its edges. A woman with folded arms stood at the bus stop in front of the building; it looked as though she was cradling a baby. Nearby, two lads nestled into each other to light cigarettes. When I looked at the woman again she was staring at me and I leaned back as if caught out at something.

Rose was playing with the dog, jiggling Jiggs in front of her. She wore a pistachio-green dress and pearls bought by her mother. My gaze went unnoticed. Why should she pay attention to me? Rose's weakness was for the opposite sex although she had lost all of her boyfriends. Her mother had thought Rose inappropriate and over-familiar with men. Rose kissed the dog's head and my silence stretched through the air.

Rose tapped the chair. 'Sit for a minute.'

I sat.

'They did mine at Missouri State Sanatorium, dearest,' she said. 'But it's no longer like past times, you must know that. In this modern world they are up-to-date with proper surgery and all. They know where to go in, where to make their mark. No drills or knives for you. They will use all their newfangled tools to remove your unhappiness.' She nodded as she spoke but her face was tight, worried-looking.

'You still have attacks, don't you?' I said.

'Petit Mal, dearest. And yes, they are a persistent memento of the nasty thing. But today is not yesterday. As I said: they go in knowing what they do.'

'It doesn't matter what they know,' I said. 'I have no choice.'

'Of course it matters, silly. I can no longer depend on myself; it would be like, as mother said, depending on a broken reed. You do not want to end up like that, like me.'

'Anything is better than the way I am,' I said.

The next day I knew it was Monday as war-torn faces hurried off to grey blocks built to keep them in. It was a struggle to envisage myself sitting amongst those desks, computers, coffee mugs, paper bins, as I had never worked. Some people have thought me idle, useless. But there was no laziness. After surgery, I knew I would be able to work, to meet new friends, to discuss how stressful it is to be busy, to be in demand. I will be wanted. For what? I didn't know. That was to be figured out when it all starts again, in the right order, in the right place.

I walked away from Dundee's wide grey water, up the hill, towards the hospital. There were tall trees, heavy with foliage, rimming the paths and pavements. Grass was richly green from the long spring rains. It had been recently mown, offering the sweet smell of what had been cut away and what was left behind. I knew I would not miss the old world as Rose has missed hers. She had not come with me. Unsurprisingly she was not fond of hospitals.

In the hospital room the sheets were smooth as snow and a large window framed the world outside. At thirty I could no longer remember a time without doctors and nurses and needles and pills. I could not remember a time when I did not shrink from the grime of a curtain or the greasy handle of a door. Now I could see a day when hours of coaching and cajoling were no longer necessary, when I would get out of bed in minutes, and it is morning instead of the middle of night, and when I would answer the phone and not discover messages from a week that had gone unnoticed.

My small suitcase sat on a chair. I knew everything inside the case. I knew how it was packed, how items were folded and compressed. I had no nervousness as I had forgotten nothing. This day had been practised well. I was on my own. Tomorrow it will be over and, yes, I will see Rose's sweet face again and tell her I am alive, at last.

This story is a work of fiction; however Rose Williams, sister of Tennessee Williams, was one of the first women in America to have a frontal lobotomy. Therefore I would like to acknowledge two texts that contributed to the making of the character of Rose: *Tennessee Williams, Notebooks*, Margaret Bradham Thornton, The University of the South,2006; and *Memoirs*, Tennessee Williams, Penguin, 2007.

Before focusing on fiction, Jane worked in higher education, writing and teaching on social work degree courses, mainly with the Open University in Scotland. She has had some non-fiction work published in relation to the rights of children in care. In the last few years Jane has written a number of short stories and has won awards from *Mslexia*, Scottish Writers' Centre and *Orange/Harper's Bazaar*. Jane has had fiction published in *Gutter* magazine and *New Writing Scotland*, and is currently writing a novel on the lives of women who have had lobotomies, including Rose Williams (sister of Tennessee) and Rosemary Kennedy. Jane lives in Fife.

Torryburn Jean

Susan MacDonald

It is easy to go back. We can all go back. Look down and begin with the shoes: shiny red with T-bar, high heel and shallow platform. Rebellious – but only slightly. Skinny ankles, spindle legs; black tights, laddered and mended with clear nail varnish beneath an A-line skirt, waistband doubled over. Look at your hands, still smooth, taking notes in rather self-conscious handwriting, the slant and downward stroke still mutating. Aladdin Sane cover on your jotter. The scent of Aqua Manda, the dragging ache of a period pain and you are there.

It is easy to go back.

Predictably, I am a little in love with Mr McDiarmid. He wears purple cords and has a faintly flamboyant quiff. My big brother knew him as Frank Ifield but now he is Tarzan. Last term when we studied *Down the Mine* Mr McDiarmid told us that his own father was sent to prison for refusing to comply with the means test. Now we are reading The Crucible.

Mr McDiarmid has placed a walking stick on his desk, highly polished wood topped with a brass carving of an owl's head. He picks it up. We fall silent. Except for Thomas Henderson who continues to chatter and snigger and leans back and stretches his legs over the sides of his chair. Hendo.

You remember Hendo. Everyone remembers Hendo. You were attracted to him or you feared him. Sometimes both. You tried to win his favour or you tried to avoid eye contact. Once a week he makes up a list of the ugliest girls in the class. Hunt the Pig. If your name appears on his list you can cry like Elaine or go red like Janet or pretend to laugh like Brenda. But you'll never feel pretty again.

"You were saying, Mr Henderson?" Tarzan waves the stick mock-menacingly in Hendo's direction. Perhaps not so mock. Hendo joins in the joke, ducks and grins appreciatively. Perhaps not so appreciatively.

Mr McDiarmid now rests the stick in his palms, horizontally, reverentially. He tells us that the stick has been in his family for over fifty years. That his grandfather acquired it from the local minister in exchange for some gardening at the manse. That it was crafted from the same piece of wood that made the stake for Torryburn Jean, the last witch to burn in Fife.

Years later, long after Tarzan has become Stone Age before retiring and opening a second-hand bookshop, I google Torryburn Jean. I find no trace.

Mr McDiarmid reads us extracts from the annals of Fife describing the suffering and torture of innocent women. The horror is somehow intensified by the use of the Scots words that I associate with my gran. I shudder. For homework, we have to write a monologue from the point of view of a woman accused of witchcraft.

At the end of the day, I giggle and gossip with my friends but the pains in my back and sides have sharpened. Limbs heavy. Hot. I head for home. Our house is in Standing Stone Walk, right at the edge of the Scheme. There is a barn beside the woods opposite. I see Brenda Gilhooley leaning against the wall, sharing a cigarette with Hendo. A murder of crows appears from the roof, wings opening like tattered umbrellas. Ziggy materialises silently, soft black fur oozing across my ankles.

I need to lie down but my gran is sleeping in my room. She is staying with us after she stumbled in her garden and broke her ankle. My brother and I spend alternate weeks on the sofa. I go to his room and lie on the bed with my knees bent, feet pushing against the wall until the spasms of pain subside. In the alien surroundings of Ewan's Black Sabbath posters, Led Zeppelin albums, guitar and sports equipment, ideas for my witch monologue begin to take shape. My eyes grow heavy as Ziggy breathes deeply beside me and I stroke the patch of white fur behind his ear.

A bell rings. My gran is awake. At times she can be what is described as 'wandered' – in the days before medical terms became household words. She complains that there are birds on her bed.

"What do you call them? Jackdaws. That's it."

I make her a cup of tea and we look at her book together: *Those Memory Years*, pictures from the 1930s. No Orwell, no miners but Little Princesses, Jack Buchanan, Gracie Fields – the singing mill girl.

"I never cared much for Gracie Fields," says Gran who was a mill girl herself. Her hands flutter like moths as she flicks away imaginary pieces of lint, the clatter of the looms still in her mind.

The next morning in registration I notice Brenda is absent. Hendo sidles to my desk, wearing his bad boy grin. He wants to copy some of my monologue because he hasn't done his homework for Tarzan. Usually I will do others' homework but this time I'm reluctant. I don't want him to see my monologue; it's too personal. Rummaging in my bag, I pretend I can't find the sheets and scribble some notes for him to copy. He is not pleased and I expect to see my name on the next 'Hunt the Pig' list.

We have a supply teacher in maths. Hendo begins a chant around the class:

"It's-Monty- Python's-Flying-Cir-CUS!"

The teacher over-reacts so Hendo twists up the ratchet:

"Tam-Pax-Tam-Pon!"

Fewer pupils join in this time and Hendo is singled out and sent to the rector to be belted. He returns, brandishing the two familiar red stripes on his palm like a badge of honour but his face is pale. At the end of the period as he passes my desk he pushes his hand against the back of my head. My hair is very dark – like a raven's wing, my gran says – but at the back I have a small blonde clump, about an inch wide. I can only see it through two mirrors, of course, but I know it's there. I reach back and touch the place where Hendo's hand has been and I discover that he has stuck chewing gum on the blonde streak. After much tugging and pulling, I remove most of the gum, but some I have to cut out with nail scissors. For many weeks, that part of my hair is ragged and uneven, but eventually it grows back, still blonde.

That night when I go home, Ziggy is missing.

My gran stares blankly at the TV, once more flicking away imaginary lint and humming a waltzy lalala tune, probably from the thirties. I work on my character study of Proctor. If I concentrate really hard, I tell myself, Ziggy will come back. It's difficult to focus, though, because a motorbike keeps roaring past our house.

"Jackdaws," says my gran.

There is still no sign of Ziggy the next day but Brenda is back at school. No laughter from her today. She is wearing lots of make-up but I'm sure I see a graze or a bruise on her cheek. When she sits down she pulls her skirt over her knees and clutches the hem. I stroke my bristly blonde streak, stare in Hendo's direction and concentrate.

That evening I have my part-time job in William Low's, stacking shelves. Tins and tins of cat food. I bump my shin against a ladder. A tiny trickle of blood sticks to my tights and, though it's not like me, I weep a little.

At home, my mum is waiting for me. She looks worried.

"Abi, Ewan found Ziggy. He was under the Donaldson's shed. It looks like, well, Ewan thinks he's been shot with an airgun. He's up at the vet's now."

For the last time in my life I am a little girl again, clinging to her mother.

An hour later, Ewan comes home alone, ashen.

Ziggy's dead.

"No, no, Abi. Ziggy's going to be all right, the vet thinks. He's stitched up his leg and his paw. Keeping him in overnight. But something terrible's happened. That Henderson boy in your class. He's been killed. Joyriding a motorbike. I can't believe it."

"His poor mother," sighs my gran as a cold, dark fear wraps itself around me...

It's easy to come back. Start with the shoes. Still red, but a matt, soft leather, the strap held in place by Velcro; thick, spongy sole. I have to wear flat shoes now because of the arthritis in my knee. And I walk with a stick. The stick my English teacher gave me the day I left school.

Crafted from the same piece of wood that was used to burn the last witch in Fife.

Susan MacDonald grew up in Fife where she lived close to a standing stone. After studying English at the University of Edinburgh, she became a teacher. She has had works published by Education Scotland and Barrington Stoke.

The Booker Man

Jayne Baldwin

No one was sure whose idea it had been, at least that was what everyone insisted later, particularly Lou who had an unsettled feeling that perhaps it was in some way her fault. No one wanted to admit they'd even made that first suggestion, however innocuous the plan had been, however harmless the whole thing had seemed. Not now; not now that it had turned out so badly, not one of the group was going to confess that the idea, brilliant and mischievous as it had been, had been theirs.

There was a brief period when several candidates were willing to quietly smile when they heard the Booker Man mentioned. Many who, if asked in whispered words over a coffee in one of the town's many bookshop cafes, would have said that yes, the local writers and artists' group had been behind the construction that had appeared mysteriously in the middle of the green.

Whoever it was that had first voiced the idea, it was so quickly taken up that it wasn't surprising that no one could really remember if one person in particular had said it. Lou certainly, if she wasn't the instigator, knew she had been the catalyst. Maggie distinctly remembered hearing the raucous laughter rolling along to her end of the table. It was inevitable that the evening should have gone this way, it always did. The writers and artists' salon held monthly at the biggest cafe in the town began each time with great intentions of seriously discussing publishing, writing and poetry over their meal but by pudding it almost always degenerated into a tipsy, if not downright drunken, conversation filled with misheard hilarities and gossip.

"Shite, it's just shite, really, don't you think so?" Helen said, putting her almost empty glass of red wine down with great care, "and," she added before anyone else could chip in with their opinion, "and, yet it's him and the likes of him that get invited every year, every bloody year. Put up at a swanky hotel and plied with claret in the writer's getaway or whatever it's called."

Helen had held up her fingers to gesture little inverted commas around the words 'writer's getaway' to emphasise her feelings about the exclusive area for authors that her change of voice had all ready indicated.

"We're all with you, hen," Lou said, "you won't find anyone to disagree with you here. Every year it's the same, hauling folk up from London, they haven't a fucking clue where they're going. Some author that one of Ms Clarke's poncy pals represents or an old Oxford chum that's written a book."

"Makes you sick, especially when she uses it to further her own career when we all know who does most of the donkey work," Fiona interjected, before continuing to enjoy her sticky toffee pudding. There were nods of agreement from everyone around their end of the table. Lou was right, for five years now the local writers had watched the town's annual book festival change from a character filled celebration of the written word to a corporate extravaganza, with fancy marquees and best selling authors. They were real crowd pullers, it had to be admitted, but the local writers, however successful, had found that their faces no longer fitted into the new director's projected festival profile.

"And what's worse," Graham said, making his point with the glass of whisky he was having instead of dessert, "they all treat the town like it's Briga fuckin' Doon. Oh how quaint the bookshops are and have you heard the way some of the locals speak, can't understand a word," he added using an accent last heard on the BBC in the nineteen-forties.

But it was somewhere within the blur of this whisky and wine fuelled exchange that the idea of the Booker Man reared it's great groggy head. Maggie's end of the table caught snippets of the ridiculous plan as the laughter rolled towards them. Linda heard 'books', 'bit o' mischief' and 'it could be massive!' float through the fumes. The plan, as it emerged through the conversation, was to build a man out of books, "the Booker Man" Linda had shrieked, followed by more guffaws from the group. Graham, as owner of the largest book shop in the town and chair of the

Chamber of Trade, knew that he could lay his hands on as many old titles as they needed. It was Graham who announced that if they used all the ones waiting to be sent away to be pulped it could be a giant.

"As we're going to have to build it in one night, without being seen, it will just have to be as big as we can make it in the time," Lou concluded.

"What about the security guard? You know, the lad that stops the local hoodies from running riot in the big marquee?" Linda asked.

"They usually employ my cousin's son, so that's not a problem," Maggie said, "and if we do it on the night they hold the trustees' meal then they'll all be too busy quaffing champagne and congratulating themselves again to notice."

"Great idea Mags," Lou smiled, "so who's in?"

In the end they'd all thought it was a great idea, not just the writers and artists group but several of the cafe staff and more than a few of the shop owners, particularly the ones who had been dropped from the festival's organising committee. It seemed there was no shortage of people in the small town who thought it would be fun to pop the hubris of the high brow literati who swanned around during the festival. The director, Paige Clarke, who now did the job from her home in Manchester after only pretending to be part of the community for the first six months, came in for particular vitriol. Patronising Paige was her unofficial nickname.

When the night arrived Graham had arranged with the book shop owners that they would have their old unsaleable stock ready to be brought out quickly. All the old books that no one wanted, pages missing, yellowed or excessively foxed, covers curled and stained. Books by out of fashion authors or so popular that thousands of copies had been printed and now, years later, they were worth little more than a penny. At first it was chaos, too many people wanting to be involved, so many that it would attract attention. Although the usually quiet town was transformed during festival time with event tents taking over from the shops and halls that had at first been used as venues, the excited gathering on the green was threatening to blow the whole thing. Fiona, the manager of the local doctors' surgery, quickly took charge and soon had some people sent off to the pub, others allocated to fetching the books and a small group tasked with building the figure. No one had thought to create a design so everyone randomly piled the books up until it started to resemble a kind of towering Frankenstein. "As seen in the films, not Mary Shelley's book," Lou pointed out. Working quickly with no regard to whether the books were heavy tomes or tattered paperbacks, the figure began to rise.

"It just has to look vaguely like a man," Helen said, "it's not an art installation after all."

But of course the next day, as the audiences started to gather for the festival's opening events, that's exactly what it was assumed to be. Despite being almost thrown together, the Booker Man actually looked pretty good, in a kind of dystopian way, he was certainly a lot bigger than they'd all expected. Once Fiona had sorted everyone out they'd all worked really well together, and in three hours they had built a rough man shaped tower of books about five feet square and nine feet tall; Graham, the tallest of them, had stood on a chair to place the last few heavy volumes to finish the rather chunky head. Someone had managed to create quite a striking nose, but, other than a heavy brow, that was the man's only facial feature. There were murmurings of delight amongst people admiring this Trojan horse that had appeared almost out of nowhere during the night. The man gazed, somewhat menacingly, towards the marquee.

"Bugger," Maggie said to some of the creative team over coffee in one of the smaller cafes the next afternoon. Their usual haunt was full of visitors as it stood opposite to the busy festival box office so they'd been forced to go round the corner to one that was less obvious and had a table free.

"I like it in here," Linda said sitting back in her chair contemplating the cakes on the counter.

"I don't mean the cafe," Maggie was a little terse, "I mean bugger, the plan's backfired. I went to have a look at the Booker Man in the daylight on the way here and I heard some people saying they think our man is part of the festival and Patronising Paige is probably, right now, being congratulated on another daring and inspired idea."

There was silence for a moment at the table as Fiona, Lou and Linda could all easily imagine the scene. Two of them had been volunteers with the festival for years and had witnessed all too often how Ms Clarke smugly soaked up the praise from some arty type in tweed suit and trilby even though she had often had little to do with the creation of the event.

They all jumped a little, brought back from their thoughts, as the bell rang on the cafe door announcing the arrival of another customer, one who was clearly discussing the Booker Man with their friend who was following them in. They were obviously from out of town.

"Marvellous, it's simply marvellous, the choice and positioning of the titles, the state of the books...it's clearly a critique on the current changes in the publishing industry..."

Lou rolled her eyes as the others all groaned or pulled faces as they overheard the comments of the two men who appeared to be thrilled with the "fabulous installation, wonder who the artist is?" One of them had already taken a photo and tweeted it "it's had ten retweets in the last five minutes," they heard him say before he asked the waitress if he could have a decaf with soya.

"You can tell she's wondering if he's speaking English," Linda said. They were all laughing at this when the door crashed open, the bell this time heralding the arrival of Helen who shouted across to the group "come now you need to see this."

This, turned out to be Paige who clearly hadn't heard that the Booker Man was being celebrated as another amazing idea and was in full flow in front of the looming figure. Clearly furious, she was berating Graham as she had quickly concluded that he was behind it.

"You must know, Graham, where all these books have come from. They're not going to appear out of thin air are they and as the chair of the Chamber of Trade only you could organise getting all these disgusting tatty old volumes together in one place so surreptitiously. Look at it! Right in the middle of the town, near the main marquee for God's sake, what an embarrassment. If I find out... " she raged.

Graham, a tall rather dour character at the best of times who was not easily intimidated, even by someone who was a mistress sneer, was still contemplating his response when Giles Gillingham, the arts correspondent for *The Times* spotted the towering figure and greeted Paige with open arms.

"Darling, it's fabulous, what a coup. Everyone's saying the artist is a secret but you must tell Giles all. You obviously commissioned it, it's got your charm, your style, what irony in this shabby figure..."

Lou thought she was going to be sick. She dragged the others away, including Graham whose wry stillness in the face of Paige's fury had now turned to astonishment as the woman began taking the credit for the Booker Man. They could hear her laughter as they left the green.

The mysterious man was the main topic of conversation in marquees, cafes and homes for the whole weekend of the festival. Rumours flew around about who had actually been behind it and what had been their motives. Pictures of the figure featured in the coverage of the festival in all the major newspapers, and in countless blogs and social media pages. It even trended on Twitter for half an hour. Giles Gillingham wrote a lengthy piece in the colour supplement about the irony and meaning of the man and what could be interpreted from the anonymity of the piece.

On the final night of the festival everyone gathered on the green to watch the firework display that traditionally brought things to a close. It was one thing that Paige hadn't changed. As the rockets fired off, Helen nudged Lou to draw her attention to the director who has leaning on the Booker Man as a photographer took some shots with the dramatic sky as a backdrop. She posed leaning back with her arms folded not realising that the figure had been hurriedly put together with no thought for health and safety. Over the three days children had pulled at it and some people had even stolen books making the whole thing even more fragile than it first was. Helen and Lou could see what was happening but they were the only ones. The crowd was looking up at the loud and colourful display, the photographer was focused on his subject and Paige was too busy posing to notice the heavy encyclopedias that made up the head were beginning to move. Lou later said that it was as if the man was peering down at Paige Clarke.

"For a moment anyway," she would say, "and then his head fell off."

It was a terrible accident of course, no one was sure whether the fatal blow had been from an old *Encyclopedia Britannica* or Paige's head striking the ground under the weight of the books or, more likely, a combination of the two. The Trustees held a memorial service and named one of the event tents after her but the festival was vital to the economy of the town so the post of director was quickly advertised and Dan, the local man who had been doing most of the work in the background anyway, was soon appointed. The following year there was quite a change. Some big names were still brought in for the headline events in the main marquee but Dan wanted to create quite a different profile for the festival and the Paige Clarke memorial tent was devoted to celebrating new and emerging writers, particularly poets and storytellers from the region.

Former newspaper reporter, Jayne Baldwin now works as a writer and children's book publisher (with a bit of yoga teaching on the side). She writes non-fiction books, children's books, flash fiction and short stories. She has had work published in a number of collections and anthologies. Her books can be found through independent and online booksellers.

African Violets

Jo Tiddy

"Sunhat, Jenny!" shouts Mummy. She's sitting on the veranda, shaded by the vines that grow up the supporting pillars.

I ignore her; I'm busy watching a trail of Siafu, staying just out of reach. The little critters bite. They're single-minded destroyers, an army snaking through the borders and across the grass. At the quarters the staff are busy putting down lines of ash, of ant-powder, to divert them.

"Jenny!"

I move out of her line of sight, further down the garden, letting the giant fig tree block her out. I'm wearing my favourite pair of shorts, and the dust coats my knees. My hair feels like straw, the result, says Mummy, of chewing the ends and too much sun. I look, according to Papa, like some deranged scarecrow. Not that I've seen one, except in books. We don't have scarecrows here. Instead, when the crows get too bold, Papa will get a rifle and shoot a few, decorating the fences around the paddocks with their corpses. It doesn't work.

"Jenny! Put your sun hat on!"

As a result of not hat wearing, I have peeling shoulders and a pink nose. I pick the dead skin off when no-one's looking. Mummy says it's a disgusting habit.

It's hot. The lawn is dotted with massive trees. They are older that the house, older even than the country, carved from the sacred forest when the lands were first cleared. Now they are islands adrift, casting dark shadows on the grass, and shading the house. The dogs lie in the puddles of shade at their bases, tongues out, panting. In the canopies, festooned with old man's beard, Turacos yell, and sometimes swoop down to nip the canna buds off.

Kimau says. "The Siafu will bring the rain, maybe." He's weeding a flower bed at the foot of the Nandi Flame, pulling away at the dead straps of the agapanthus leaves and stabbing at the rock hard soil to get at the weeds. He smiles up at me. Before I can speak he's moved off, trundling the heavy barrow with its squeaky wheel.

The rains are late. A month late now. Each morning towers of cloud spawn out beyond the Rift, bellies pregnant with the promise of salvation. By noon they have dissipated, dissolved back into the blue. All that remains is white light and dust, a holding of breath, and a gardener's prayer. Even in the garden the earth smells scorched, despite the watering rota, and the red-chested cuckoo sings outside my window every morning: "It will rain, it will rain". He lies. The ponds, the dam by the quarters, are shrinking, water seeping away through the black cotton soil. Kimau waters the big pots on the veranda; these stay lush and green, while the lawns slowly yellow. He deadheads the collection of African Violets that Mummy cultivates so carefully and displays on an old sewing table. Purple and pink and blue, like faded jewels. I watch him move slowly through his allotted list of jobs, pushing the ancient mower; he's slick with sweat. Where the lawn turns to paddock he slashes pathways through the grass with a wicked looking panga, sharp as sin. I follow him, picking up treasures exposed on the ground to show him; a piece of obsidian, a turaco feather, red on black, once, a snake skin outgrown by its owner.

At the weekends I'm out all day, won't come home until the sun sinks. I'm on my bike, with the other kids along the Ridge, or trekking through the rides and thickets of the Ololua Forest. It's cooler in the forest, and there is always the fear that we'll get lost, swallowed up. When I get home the woodsmoke is curling up from the staff quarters, the night askari is guarding the big gate and the dogs are being fed slabs of meat before being let loose to run the fences and hedges that keep us safe. The sun sinks behind the knuckles of the Ngongs, the hazy hills a backdrop to the sweeping main lawn. Last rays of sunlight catch the Bird of Paradise flowers planted in the long border, they are colourful dinosaur heads rearing out of the foliage below. Erica is setting tea on the table.

"Eh toto kidogo, you hungry? Wash your hands." Erica has set tea on the table. She watches as I wolf it down. Erica smells of Mansion floor wax and stale sweat, comforting. On Tuesdays, Erica polishes acres of red tile and parquet, on her knees applying the wax. The best bit is after, when Erica straps sheepskin pads to her feet and glides over the floors buffing them to a shine. I try it sometimes, it's harder than it looks.

"We're going out darling." Mummy is always going out, there are bridge parties, supper clubs, the theatre to visit. I am tucked up with a cup of Milo by Erica, who sits in the empty house until my parents come home. They're always very late.

Nights in Africa are not silent. There is the screeching of night jars, and of monkeys. There is the thousand-fold creaking of frogs in the ornamental ponds and the storage dams. There is the cough of a leopard, venturing out of the Forest onto the Ridge in search of easy dinners. The farm up the road employs armed askaris to protect the horses. The night noises are my lullaby. Any change, a sudden silence, or the barking of dogs, will wake me , will wake the whole house. Then Papa will go for the guns, Mummy will stand ready to hit the siren that will bring the neighbours and the response unit. Every house on the ridge has this system. Every house has big dogs, kept hungry. Every house has high fences, has strong bars welded onto the windows to prevent the darkness getting in.

In the early evenings, if Papa is home, he gets the little .22 out of the gun cupboard and teaches me to shoot. We stand together on the lawn. Cans line the fenceposts by the pasture. He shows me how to load, sight, squeeze. The recoil gets me every time, but I'm used to it now.

"That's my girl." I bask in Papa's approval.

"Do you have to?" Mummy drawls from the veranda, on her second gin and tonic. "It makes such a racket." Sundowner time is when Mummy can sit back and admire her garden, all her hard work. Tendrils of jasmine unfurl their heavy scent into the evening air. I can smell it from here, as I raise the .22 to my eye and knock another can off.

"Oh hush woman, it's a useful skill."

"Well hurry up, we're due at the Johnsons for drinks."

"Bugger," says Papa, but quietly. He gives my shoulder a squeeze.

I don't move, I live for these moments with Papa. I'm going away to school when I turn eleven, and the thought is a scabbed sore to pick at, until I think I will cry and cry. I won't though.

When the rains finally break it is a relief. Water hammers on the corrugated roof and drips runnels into the dry earth below. I can almost see the plants growing, the cannas throw off their dusty mantles, their striped leaves glow. The garden is transformed, it smells of damp, of the forest from which it was hacked. I sleep to the lullaby of rain, it drowns out all other sounds. When I wake it is still raining.

In the garden Mummy is frantic, She has Kimau staking, clearing away detritus, branches and leaves brought down by the rain. He digs channels to divert the torrent of water that threatens to food the flowerbeds. The bougainvillea that scrambles over the main gate is in tatters, its Fanta orange flowers drooping like crumpled paper, dissolving in the deluge. The hills beyond are shrouded in low cloud, and still it rains, big fat drops that soak you through in moments. The rose bed is ruined. Mummy is keen on her roses, but they don't grow so well here.

"No, not like that. Like this". There's an edge to Mummy's voice that reminds me of when Mary left. I liked Mary. She didn't get cross when I left my clothes on the floor, just smiled at me and shook her head as she picked them up. She was caught stealing from the sugar supply in the store cupboard.

"I will not have a thief in the house." Mummy had yelled. I hid in my room, when Mummy's in this mood its best to keep out of her way. Mary left without even saying goodbye.

Mummy is shouting now, as Kimau tries to disentangle himself from the ruin of the roses. Kimau looks at her, silent, as blood drips down his arm from the thorns. The sun has come out, and steam rises from the lawn.

"Just sort it out, OK?" Mummy throws down the secateurs and storms inside. I bring Kimau a plaster from the first aid box. His arm is muscled and hard, the blood bright against his skin.

Mummy goes out for her weekly game of golf, and Max from along the Ridge comes over to play. His house is even bigger than ours, and his parents have two gardeners, a fact that Mummy mentions often. We're

49

not interested in the garden though, we just want to play football. Erica is supposed to be keeping half an eye on us, but she's got a mountain of ironing to get through, so is in the dhobi room at the back of the house. We've already squashed the bed of Marguerites and African Daisies, so Max has the bright idea of using the posts of the veranda as a goal. We lug the chairs around to protect the windows at the back.

It's a great game. For once I am doing better than Max, who is getting sulky. Five-two, and it's my turn again. I kick hard, aiming right at Max. I miss; instead the ball, newly pumped up by Kimau, skews sideways into the table of African Violets, knocking it over and smashing the pots.

"Oh shit." says Max.

I cannot even breathe. I am going to be in so much trouble. We spend the rest of the afternoon in the far paddock, well away from the house. We hide the football.

There is an almighty shauri when I finally return. Mummy is shouting, Kimau is silently sweeping up the shards of terracotta and wilted plants. He looks at me, I look at the floor. I say nothing.

Kimau is dismissed. The table of violets was the last straw, Mummy says; she can't believe it was mere carelessness on his part. He hasn't been working hard enough, Mummy says; he's answered back too many times. He stands, mute, as Papa pays him off. No reference. He's to be out of the quarters by the end of tomorrow.

I can see the scorn in Kimau's eyes as he holds out his hand to take the money, a week's wages, no more. I hope he finds another job soon, I hopes he forgets us, me. Papa asks if I want to practice my shooting again, but I shake my head. There's a wiggle of shame in my belly, and I go to bed early.

Two nights later, when it's properly dark, one of the dogs gets taken. There's a snarling from the darkness, which turns to howls, then silence. The other dogs come whining in from the garden, and Papa races out shining a flashlight into the kai apple hedge that separates us from the wilderness. He harangues the night askari, who just stands there, head down. It is possible that he has been asleep on duty. It is possible he was looking the other way. The staff have been sullen since Kimau left. Even Erica no longer smiles as she sets tea on the table.

"I saw nothing, bwana," says the askari.

There is no trace of Boris, just a hole in the fence and a little blood on the grass. I do cry at that, he was a friendly soul, would follow me around the paths and paddocks south of the house, or flomp at my feet as I stretched out on the lawn with a book. Papa just grunts.

"Leopard maybe. It happens. Here, blow."

Mummy whispers. "Do you think...? Remember the Boomes?"

"Ssh," says Papa, looking sideways at me, and he changes the subject. I know who they're talking about: my friend Deborah from down the Ridge. Her dogs were poisoned one night. Then her dad was shot, with his own gun. The police thought it was one of the staff, but they never charged anyone. The family left for England the following week, just packed up and went, no goodbyes. For months after that Mummy was jumpy in the evenings.

"Go to bed, pumpkin," Papa says. I can't sleep though. Outside, in the garden, darkness is coiled.

When I get up early next morning, Papa is asleep in the big chair in the living room, by the remains of the dead fire. The big gun is resting across his knees. Light from the windows scatters across the room. The birds sing, "It will rain, It will rain."

We see a leopard later that week. It's lit up in the headlights as we drive home late along the Ridge, a rippling menace that glares at us momentarily, then stalks into the darkness. It's the most beautiful thing I've ever seen and a fraction of my heart forgives it for the dog. I hope it was the leopard.

"That's it then," says Papa, and his shoulders relax just a little. Nonetheless, he keeps the rifles loaded. Just in case.

Jo Tiddy spent an idyllic childhood in Kenya, living at the coast, and then on the outskirts of Nairobi, close to where Karen Blixen had her coffee farm. She moved back to the UK in the mid 1980s and was horrified to discover how cold it was! Innumerable years were spent working for local government as a Planner, and later a Heritage Officer, and Jo still has an unhealthy obsession in ridding the world of uPVC windows. She currently works part time in a primary school, patching grazed knees and sorting out minor wars.

Jo has been writing for two years, has won the inaugural Thame Short Story Competition which was very encouraging, was recently one of the winners of the Mumsnet/Walker Books Animal Stories competition and has been shortlisted in a few writing competitions.

She lives in Thame, Oxfordshire with her long-suffering husband, two daughters and a very large dog.

Tunnel of love

Nancy McKnight

I won't ever run to catch a train. I'm always afraid the damn thing moves off as I'm stepping aboard, and I'll be dragged along till there's nothing left except a blood-soaked scrap of raincoat, a disembodied hand clutching the handle. Or I'll slip down into the space between the carriage and the edge of the platform and be crushed to a pulp on the greasy concrete sides. So all my life I've missed trains rather than run.

Ewan is familiar with this foible. Consequently, he makes a point of depositing me at least twenty minutes early at the station dropping-off point. Dropping-off. That's what I feel I'm doing to them, as I grab my bag, wave to Josh and turn my back. I can stroll to the platform at my leisure, because Ewan has bought my ticket seven days in advance, to save money. I am cavalier with his money now. I buy *National Geographic* in WH Smith, so that Marcella will think I passed the journey reading. It is rarely now that I am permitted to make this visit without Josh.

The last scrap of my everyday, boring life drops off, sloughed like a snake's skin. I do not need to be Faye Dunlop for another two and a half hours, I'm not Josh's mother, or a housewife, or the proprietrix of a four -bed-detached-executive-home-with-a-cat-and-a-dog, or Marcella's sister-in-law.

It wasn't always like this. In the early days we were reckless. Entire Thursdays were spent in a first-floor bedroom in the Holyrood Hotel, always the same one. It had a small iron balcony, and French windows, and white muslin curtains that billowed in the breeze. Even in November, we left the windows open. The heat of our bodies was sufficient.

I see him as soon as I start walking down the platform. I always notice his hair first, the dark mystery of it I could lose my soul in, and his perfect ears which lie neat and close against his skull like an exotic animal's, the skin of them the colour of butterscotch. He's sitting with his eyes closed, a slight smile lifting the corners of his finely-drawn mouth. He's ageing much better than I am. Men always do. He has such exquisite bones. That perfect nose, that hawk's profile – he'll keep these when he's eighty, his beauty will remain intact till he dies. He'll be an exquisite corpse.

He opens his eyes suddenly (no matter how often, I'm still unprepared for the amber warmth in them), and gives me an imperceptible wave, while I smile vaguely and walk on. Not too far. Not as far as the next carriage.

I resent every one of the six hundred seconds before the doors jerk shut and the whole contraption lurches into motion. I keep my eyes closed and start to count backwards from three hundred. I've only reached ninety-seven when I sense him at my shoulder and slip across into the window seat. I feel him slide in beside me and glide his fingers round mine in one graceful motion.

"Mmmm," he sighs, as he always does, "a warm seat!"

And I grin, as I always do, and turn my face to get a kiss, even though it isn't time yet.

He spreads his jacket over his knees.

"How are you?" He sounds so different in the flesh, compared to over a phone line. His voice is deeper, it has more body. It seems to come from inside my own head. "God! It's so good to have you to myself for a couple of hours."

It's more than six months since we had a Thursday afternoon in the hotel. Eight weeks since he was daring enough to play a stranger, arriving at my elbow as I trailed Josh round the Islamic Pottery section of the second-floor gallery in the museum. My son didn't notice my sharp intake of breath. Jav did, though. He teased me about it later, on the phone.

"I thought I could only get you to do that with a rather more intimate contact than touching your elbow," he said. "Do it again, so I can dream."

I'd been gazing at the inimitable blue of a seventeenth-century plate, when I felt that lightest of touches, and that voice that can make my heart stop said: "They used cobalt mined near Kashan to get that shade. And iron to produce the green in that water-pipe."

"I like the blue best," I said huskily.

"Probably produced in Isfahan. You know where that is?"

And he pointed it out on the wall-map beside the case. "Perhaps you'll visit it one day," he said.

"I'm bored," whined my son. "I want a drink." (I experienced an inrush of Lady Macbeth sentiment; if only there had been a stone of the dashing-out-brains variety handy).

"Then we must find you a drink, my friend," said Jav, and he took us to the museum cafeteria, and bought Josh Coke and ice cream, and chatted to him with an ease that broke my heart, for all the time, I was picturing him with his own two boys; the younger is exactly Josh's age.

I try not to think about that, normally. But all that was showing at the cinema in my head was Javad-the-Perfect-Father, and it was more painful to watch than the imagined images of him with his wife.

Josh clyped, of course. "He talked to Mummy about old china," he said. "But he has a Rolex watch, and he bought me a double scoop of chocolate."

Ewan only flashed me the faintest flicker of suspicion.

But I don't have to think about children for the next two and a half hours, not anyone's children. (My mind's watching him playing cricket with his boys, on a sandy beach identical to the one in the travel poster at the end of the carriage). He'll never leave them.

"Hey," he says, "why so pensive? We have this small time together, my love. Let's not waste a second of it on sad thoughts."

My love. He's rarely spoken the word to me, though in the early days – before the train journeys or the hotel or the furtive and brief phone conversations, in the days when we were just two people with the keyword "ceramics" in their member profiles – it had crept into the closing lines of our e-mails. Open, read, delete, empty recycle bin. Start menu – settings – clear document list. Sigh. Shut down computer. All that electronic love denied and consigned to the ether. My love. In his language, as well as in English, we wrote it. I'm like a soldier; all I know of this exotic language that's his native tongue are the words for food and weather and emotions and bodily pleasures.

His hands are always warm, even in winter. By Dunbar, his arm will be round my shoulders too, my head leaning against his. By the time the refreshment trolley's completed its first pass, we'll be gazing into one another's eyes like teenagers.

How did we get caught up in this, why have we swallowed the lie about 'for the sake of the children'? We're young enough to know better.

I pray for the tunnels (travelling in the opposite direction is heart-breaking, because there's the Haymarket tunnel, then it's Waverley already, and the kiss is the parting kiss and it's all over).

At the first tunnel, his mouth will seek mine. I particularly love his mouth, and the firmness of his lips that press mine open to the caress of his tongue.

His hair has a sprinkling of silver at the temples now. It makes me faint and nauseous to see that; we've spoken in vague terms of the time when the children are grown, when they're old enough. We're ageing too. We may be too old. The Thursday afternoon fire won't burn forever.

"Look!" He nudges me. "There's another few slates off. The price is coming down all the time."

It's the first of 'our' houses. There are another six, and over the past twenty months we've bought them and moved into caravans in overgrown gardens and replaced slipped slates and rotten timbers with our own hands, working side by side, so close our fingers touch as I hand him slates, nails, hammer. We've ordered new windows (after much argument, I've prevailed; red cedar they shall be, for they have to last for the rest of our lives, damn the expense). I know exactly where in each identical kitchen the blue Aga will sit, I feel the warmth from it on my face, as I look through the red-cedar-framed window at the garden full of bluebirds and daffodils and cherry blossom. I fall asleep dreaming of the colour of the walls of the bedroom where I'll lie every night in Javad's arms.

"Won't the trains keep us awake?" he'd said the first time.

"They'll rock us to sleep."

All of 'our' houses are isolated. We won't need neighbours, only one another, and a huge pine bed in the upstairs room with sloping ceilings and deep turquoise, under-the-sea blue walls. Without neighbours we'll be able to love each other as noisily as we want (and with him, I've always wanted to be very noisy indeed). It's so long since I saw him other than fully-clothed. But during the kisses (even in short tunnels) I can feel. Oh, yes!

A passing woman apologises as the train lurches and throws her against Jav. She smiles indulgently at us.

"I've seen you before, haven't I?" she says. My blood chills. "I remember saying to my pal I'd seen such a glamorous couple on the train, the woman as blonde as an angel and her husband tall dark and handsome, just like film stars, and the pair of them crazy in love with each other." She squeezes Jav's shoulder, and continues on her way, cackling.

"Don't," he whispers. "She's just a stupid old woman. Nothing to be sad about, Faye, I can't bear it when you're sad. It'll be true, one day soon. They're getting older every day."

"So are we," I say bitterly. "And once they are grown – what'll your excuse be then?"

He looks at me despairingly. That was a mean thing to say. He's never been anything other than faithful to our fantasies. He presses his mouth down on mine, even though we aren't in a tunnel.

"I love you," he says. "Maybe we have to find another way. Maybe we have to harden our hearts."

Mine almost stops. Harden them against whom?

"I find it harder to bear every day," he says. "If you feel like that too, perhaps we have to think less about the children."

"But she'd never let you take the boys, would she?" Any more than Ewan would let me have Josh. And somehow, that matters less to me just now.

"No."

"Then you'd be miserable. You'd blame me. We'd be fighting in less time than it would take to put the roof right."

"Don't let's fight now then, sweetheart. We have so little time."

We break off the clinch to refuse the offer of tea, coffee, soft drinks, gin, beer, wine, whisky, sandwiches, shortbread or crisps.

I'm thinking of something I read yesterday, wondering if he'd seen it too, a couple fined for joining the mile-high club without making it to the usual facilities. One of the witnesses said she only realised what was happening in front of her when the woman's foot, still in red stiletto, came over the back of the seat. If the paper was right about the amount of booze they'd shifted, and considering the leg-room in economy class, I thought it was quite an achievement. You could never do that on a train. Too many people coming and going, too many house windows twenty metres from the track. Like ours.

But I find I want Javad more than I can recollect wanting anyone before. My body feels as if it's melting like candle wax, it'll drip down over the edge of the seat and run across the floor. He shifts his jacket on his lap. He wants me too.

There's always the toilet? I saw that in a film once, only it was gay men, one of them bent over the basin, with his nose squashed against the glass, like a kid making faces at a window.

I shudder. They stink to high heaven anyway, and there are too many rails and knobs and traps for the unwary. Too many wee buttons that control the door lock and the door opener, in these fancy new trains.

"Jav…" I say.

"I know, my love. I know."

I fight to switch off my imagination. Another two hours and he can be back in Newcastle with her, he can fling her down on their bed and get it out of his system. Men can do that. Even if I was in bed with Ewan right now, this instant, I could never, ever shut my eyes and pretend. I've tried.

"Bloody hell!" Jav says suddenly.

My eyes shoot open. "What's wrong?"

"Look."

It's our fifth house, the one I've always held out most hope for (in my dreams, he keeps his job in the hospital in Newcastle, as if nothing has happened). Its roof is red pantile rather than slate, and there's the

58

sweetest little burn at the side of its garden, and a grove of apple and plum trees I itch to prune.

"Oh, my God, no!"

The grass has been churned up by machinery, and two white transit vans are parked on the lawn. All the roof-tiles are off and stacked. As we whisk past, workmen are lifting on new roof-trusses.

We part at York in silence, like strangers coming from a funeral. Normally, we don't even risk walking up the platform together, because Marcella comes in to meet me. This time, it doesn't seem to matter. We make polite and desultory conversation about how East Coast have improved their time-keeping.

"When will you be travelling again?"

"I'm not sure. I'll e-mail you."

"Who was that?" says Marcella. She's looking more and more like Ewan as she gets older. They both take after their mother.

"Oh, I don't know. Some man who was on the train."

Marcella rolls her eyes, and pats her hair. "Handsome! Some sort of Arab?"

"I suppose he could be."

"Full of Eastern promise. These sort of dark eyes turn me on. How's my darling bro, then, and the brat?"

Glasgow-born Nancy McKnight lives in Galloway, and has worked as a journalist (under the name of Fiona Cameron) and lecturer, as well as a PR/marketing consultant. Several of her short stories have been published in *New Fiction* anthologies, and she is shortly due to launch *Containment*, the second book in the *Balvaig Trilogy*.

The Wood

Tina Waterman-Roberts

"Thank God, it's Sunday!" Jess had not set the alarm and had woken late. She stretched her arms above her head and then frowned as she suddenly had a feeling that something was wrong. It was not, however, until she swung her feet out of bed and stared down that she became aware of exactly what it was that was wrong. She gaped in horrified fascination at her feet, which were covered in small, over-locking scales pointing down towards her five toes which were splayed and thickened, ending in black talons which curved to sharp points. Jess screamed, but nothing changed. She screamed again, then, gradually, tried to flex her toes while trembling and clutching the bed head. The talons responded, clenching and relaxing. They could not be her feet. Her feet were Jimmy Choo feet - slim, elegant and pedicured.

She gasped: "But... wha...what has happened?" she asked the bedroom. Rushing into the bathroom, she leapt into the bath and began rubbing vigorously, trying to rid her feet of the ghastly scales. This had no effect, so Jess ran into the kitchen and grabbed the bleach from under the sink. Back in the bathroom she began scrubbing at the scales with the bleach and a nailbrush, growing more and more frantic, finally trying to scrape them off with her fingernails. Her hands grew tired and red, there was a faint tingling in her feet, but the scaly growths remained.

"What am I to do?" Jess began crying, "I can't bear it." She wandered round the house in her bathrobe, the talons clicking on the wooden floors. Jess picked up her phone, hesitated and put it down again. She thought of the people she knew, people who worked for her, the few women with whom she would go shopping and have the occasional coffee, the people she called friends.

"I can't tell anyone," she thought. "How can I explain what's happened? No-one would understand, they'd just disown me." She thought of the ridicule and gossip that would ensue and the sneers and comments of 'just deserts' that would follow any sharing of her predicament. Jess went back to her bedroom and opened the wardrobe. She looked at the range of beautiful, high-heeled shoes. The shoes she loved and always wore. She sat on the bed and cried again.

The rest of Sunday passed in a haze, Jess alternating between crying and getting very drunk. Towards the end of the day, she began to think about Monday and work.

"How can I go to work? What will they all say?" She thought of her staff, staff whom she never failed to put down with derision when their appearance did not, in her estimation, measure up to her own exacting standards in all respects; staff whom she had, occasionally, and with some satisfaction at the time, provoked to tears.

"They all hate me anyway," she wailed, "Now I'm like this, how will they react?" The reaction of others had always been an important criterion to Jess. She enjoyed showing her superiority in dress sense. How could she go into work with these things on her feet? She couldn't wear the beloved high heels or the short shirts which showed off her long legs to advantage. But, how could she not go into work? She had studied hard for her qualifications and worked all the hours there were to be in a position to set up her own beautician's. She couldn't trust the staff to carry out their roles properly unless she was there to oversee every moment and, besides, she desperately needed the money to pay off the mortgage, especially since she'd lost her house-mate.

She looked round wildly until her eyes lighted on the boots pushed to the back of the wardrobe that Shelley had inadvertently left behind when, after what Jess thought of as kindly comments to help Shelley make more of herself, the woman had stormed out of the house. She had come back later to collect her things, but had forgotten the boots. Jess tried on the large fur-lined boots and, to her relief, they fitted over the claws, though she felt they looked dreary and not at all the sort of thing she would wear.

The next morning she found an old pair of trousers. After all, she could hardly wear a short skirt with these boots, but trousers might hide them a bit. She couldn't seem to find anything to match. Strangely, all the coloured tops in her wardrobe seemed to have lost their brightness and to be merging into a sort of grey, so she chose the first thing that came to hand and, with red-rimmed eyes, got into the car and drove to work. As she passed through the wood that bordered the narrow land leading from her house to the main road, she shivered, rather theatrically, she admitted to herself. But she found the wood bleak and the overhanging trees rather threatening. She had once ventured in, shortly after moving to the house, but hadn't penetrated far as she was afraid that, once out of sight of the road, she would lose herself among the spindly trees and thick undergrowth vying for the light. Altogether, she thought it a dark and depressing place.

She drove into the car park and taking a deep breath, opened the door of her beautician's. She saw the surprised looks on the staff's faces and said stiffly: "Chilblains." As she went to her office, she heard the sniggers behind her back. Her hearing seemed to have improved and she could hear the comments and giggles as she left the staffroom.

"Well, who'd have thought we'd see her in trousers and flat boots."

"Doesn't she look a sight?" No-one sympathised or asked her how she was feeling. The day passed slowly and Jess continued to find that colours dimmed, although she could see everything in sharp relief. Finally, it was time to close the shop. Jess couldn't wait to get home, but on her way to the car, she hesitated by the butchers' shop.

"I don't like red meat." she said to herself, puzzled, but found herself inside, ordering lamb chops. As she drove home, she was surprised that the cars coming towards her kept flashing her. "I can see perfectly well. What's the matter with them?" she spoke angrily. Ignoring other car drivers, she turned into the small lane, leading past the large wood to her house. Whereas before the wood had seemed to be a gloomy mass, now she found that she could glimpse some movement among the trees, perhaps it was a small animal rustling in the brushwood.

Once inside her house, Jess muttered to herself: "I've got to see if they've gone," and went into the bedroom and stripped off. What she saw in the mirror frightened her. Her once slim thighs had become thicker and more muscular, her shoulders seemed hunched, while her eyes appeared to have moved towards the sides of her face and her once pert nose had elongated. "What am I?" she moaned. She covered herself up in her bath robe.

Going back to the kitchen she grabbed the chops and shoved them into a frying pan. Suddenly, Jess found herself standing next to the cooker in the immaculate kitchen, rather than sitting at the neatly laid place at the table gripping a chop in her hands and tearing at it with her teeth. The blood from the under-cooked meat ran down her chin and dripped onto the white-tiled floor.

Jess gave a strangled cry and dropped the chop. She looked at her hands where the skin was becoming loose over the bones and wrinkling and beginning to overlap her knuckles. She could trace the lines of the tendons back to her wrists and her fingers were curling over her palms while her nails had lengthened. She dropped to the floor and, rocking back and forwards, uttered incoherent cries.

Eventually, she made her way to her bedroom, then couldn't remember why she had gone there. Everything looked strange. She grabbed a handful of clothes and flung them out of the wardrobe, her now sharp nails catching and tearing the delicate fabrics. She kicked at the rows of shoes and scattered them on the floor. Moving her head slowly from side to side she tried to enunciate her feelings, but no words came, just inarticulate sounds.

Leaving the front door wide open, Jess ran out of the house and towards the end of the garden. She crouched under a tree and whimpered softly to herself. Looking down, she caught sight of the talons on her toes, gleaming black in the gathering gloom. The scales on her feet were a blue-green shade and glistened. Jess put out a tentative hand, now also scaly, and stroked her feet. The scales felt warm and smooth under her touch. She stayed like that for some time.

At last she stood up, her bathrobe slipped off, but she ignored it and didn't seem to feel the cold of the autumn evening. Jess hesitated for a few moments, then felt herself drawn down the drive towards the lane. She knew she was searching for safety and loped softly towards the dark wood.

Tina has been writing for some years, but has recently moved from the academic area of women's role in technology. Retirement has given her more time and she draws inspiration from the Galloway countryside and its history. Encouraged by the Booktown Writers, she has progressed to short stories which she finds more rewarding.

Bull Moose Cabin

Jo Mulkerrin

Bull Moose Cabin

Tuesday, September 5

Dear Forrest

It's dull today, and I'm in no mood for writing. The clouds rolled across soon after dawn, bringing with them melancholy. 'Hello old friend,' I say, 'good to see you again.' I'm hoping I'll fool it into thinking I haven't been waiting, that I am surprised to see it. But it knows better, and just makes itself comfortable, puts it's feet on the table, and stretches out. No use hoping I can keep it at bay. I am pretty poor at that. We settle down together and hope it will rain. By now you'll be wondering if it's worth reading on. Well, yes, as a matter of fact it is, as I have some news. When you were last here, do you remember me showing you old Pacey's pitch? Down from Nimpo Lake, about half a kilometre from the Viewpoint. He was out the back when we drove by, so you didn't get to see him. (Did you really have to go?) I was up at Dot's bakery yesterday, getting pizza and those great little multi grain rolls she's so good at. There was a crowd in there, and I hate it when I have to be pleasant, make conversation, or at least register some level of interest in their small talk. But just this once, there was something worth listening to. It seems the police were up at Pacey's last Friday (you left Wednesday?) Seems Jameson had seen them just after night started up. They had flashlights, and a couple of dogs. No barking or anything, just like they

65

were looking for something around the back. Jameson thought it was just them looking for that rogue cougar, and he expected them to be finding Pacey half eaten, or something. By the time Jameson was on his way back from settling the horses, they had gone. It all looked like normal, the front porch light on and all. He says he thought nothing of it and went back home. Didn't even mention it to Agnes, this was the first she'd heard of it, and she let him know it for the entire store to hear. Bet she paid for that when they got home.

Bull Moose Cabin

I remember Pacey when he first settled up here. No one seemed to know where he'd come from. He just arrived, along with his scrawny little wife, and her with a babe on her hip. Seemed friendly enough, although I almost never got to see her - only once when the doctor was up and she was in line, and again walking the road down to Meredith last summer, picking berries from the scratchy bushes.

It's rare I feel like I want to commune, but I saw in Pacey a sort of kindred spirit. It was as if we shared a similar load, as if we could understand one another, and maybe he'd be the nearest I could call a friend. He wasn't really old, (do you remember me telling you any of this? Were you listening?) Probably in his forties, but he was like an old timer. He worked all the day hacking and shaping his logs, making dog kennels and the like which he sold up on his road front for next to nothing. He'd sit out there with his pipe, his legs wide with sharp knees pressing through his threadbare overalls. That's when I'd catch up with him, and we'd pass a few words. Like me he didn't like to hold a gaze, so I could perch on his step, listening, but not looking at his words, and he'd do likewise. His profile was like his knees, all angles, and his ears poking through his hanging, greasy hair. But with life being the way it is, the communing slowed. Perhaps we didn't need to sit by each other any more.

Glad to say it's started to rain, and I am reassured. Melancholy and me, we can light the stove now.

So, on with the story. On Monday, Jameson had reason to go into town to re-register his guns, and met up with Bull Graham. He was on the desk at the licensing office, and had just been to the Courthouse, to open up. There he read the list of prisoners up in court this week, and saw the name. Sorrel Pacey. That's a pretty name don't you think? On further investigation, Bill found out that things were not what they seemed. Old Pacey had brought with him not his wife, but his daughter.

Bull Moose Cabin

Young Sorrel Pacey, at fifteen, had fallen pregnant by her pa, her mom being dead from too much baby carrying. He had upped sticks and moved to Nimpo with Sorrel, baby in tow, as soon as she turned sixteen, passing the girl off as his wife, and the babe as his own. He carried on messing with the girl, making her pregnant again. This time she couldn't take it, and after she'd borne it she put it in a plastic bag tied up tight, and buried it. Told him Min at the drugstore had it for a few days to give her a rest. Pacey found it a week on when digging over for fall planting. She hadn't dug deep, no strength I suppose, just a covering. Once Bull understood, he thought it odd that Pacey reported her to the police. Didn't he have any notion of what that could lead to? But you know this place, like as not I reckon the police wouldn't want to know. Anyway, they came up to collect the babe's body and took Sorrel away. The other child was sent somewhere else, who knows where.

I wonder if I should have known. Why I hadn't enquired of the girl. And I worry what I saw in him that made me feel akin. I can see you now, reading this and thinking "the woman's nuts. She should move away, get a grip and stop this solitary life." But you left me here, and here I'll stay. And if you were closer, you would hear my sigh.

Well, the stove's up to heat, the coffee's on, and my erstwhile friend and I have a little way to go before bedtime.

Yours ever,
May

Jo wrote Bull Moose Cabin whilst staying on a remote homestead in northern Canada. It is her first published story. She is currently working on her first novel, writing with quiet menace of the claustrophobic world of a London prison. Using the experience of her career as a Probation Officer, she delves into the darker side of people's lives, and the redemptive power of truth. Jo lives in the Highlands with her husband in their self-built house, and finds her inspiration in the stark contrast of her writing with the peace and beauty her surroundings offer.

Mother Water

Anni Telford

The interior of the Kaplumbağa bar is always dark. When you come in out of the constant dazzle that is Gabon's sun you just have to pause a moment for your eyes to adjust. He's doing just that, a young hero, all tan and sun bleached hair, another sensation seeker who thinks he'll find a meaning for his life in equatorial Africa. He's asking Mba Nze something and the old man points down the bar, points in my direction. Bintou sends them to the Kaplumbağa, tells them I'm the man to speak to for wild stories about the sea and Africa. They pull up a stool...mine's a pint of Régab and a large rum chaser. It's usually their first visit and they don't come back even though Gabon is beautiful, especially here at the edge of the Mayumba National Park. The beach stretches for long miles. I walk the sands at night when palm trees rustle in the pre-dawn breeze and the tide is rising. You can hear mongoose and genet foraging for their next meal in the undergrowth at the top of the beach and on the tide line ghost crabs scuttle to and fro in time with the rhythmic wash, picking tasty morsels from damp sand. When the moon's dark, when the predators are blinded, the leatherbacks come ashore to lay their eggs. Gabon is a magnet for leatherbacks, they swim along the equator, drawn to their rookeries on its white sands. But the young bucks don't want to hear about turtles, they want to hear about Mamiwata. Bintou says the Mamiwata has cursed me, I say I have been blessed.

Eight winters I've been coming here, to Gabon, looking for her, even caught sight of her one December night 'couple of years ago. Muriel; know what the name means? It's from the Gaelic, Muireall, means sea bright. A beautiful name for a gorgeous creature. Here in Gabon they call her Mamiwata, but she's one and the same. The Bwiti, the animists, take iboga to see her, but you don't need hallucinogenics; if you're lucky, if she wants you, she'll be waiting for you down on the beach. How did it all start? Well, my glass is empty and I'd better be getting off home. Another? But that's very kind.

It started in late summer, in Scotland, South West Scotland to be exact. Pete and I were heading out to a film location, on our way to Drummore, a village on Luce Bay. I was fighting the wheel of the Landrover as it twisted its way up the coast road, wipers struggling to clear the rain. We were both straining forward, trying to see the road in the storm gloom. We struggled on until the headlights picked out some houses clinging to the side of the road against the storm surge crashing white over a harbour wall, then the welcoming sight of the Mariner's Hotel. Staggering into reception, carrying our bags and underwater cameras, we shook the rain from our hair and the stiffness from our legs. The woman in reception was striking, green eyes, pale skin, hair as dark and shiny as an oil slick on an Atlantic swell. I could tell from Pete's face that her slow smile had the same effect on him as it had on me. She welcomed us to the hotel, introduced herself as Muriel and favoured Pete with a smile; jealousy stirred in my guts. Then she looked directly into my eyes, gave me the same treatment and the jealousy was immediately replaced with the warm flush of arousal. Her eyes were incredible, the clear green you find in the seas off the Arctic ice shelf. I think I managed to answer her questions without looking a complete fool. We were on assignment for Nature Television, filming leatherback turtles, all expenses paid and I tried to beam a mental thank you back to the woman in our office who picked the accommodation.

Muriel handed us our keys, pointed out the stairs, bar and restaurant. Neither of us paid much heed to what she was saying, we were just too busy looking at her to hear. We carted our kit up the narrow stairs, the sign over the front door had read 1642, way before lifts but we were both grinning, both thinking the same. I dropped my kit outside room fourteen, Pete was in the one opposite. That's when we made the bet; a pony for the first one to score with the miraculous Muriel. Now don't get me wrong, this was not my usual style. Pete yes, he was always chasing skirt, but not me. I was a one girl guy, in a serious relationship, of the live in type. I was even having a few thoughts about becoming a family guy.

After dinner, in the bar, Pete and I settled down before the log fire and a couple of young hobby divers joined us. I sipped at a Laphroig and chilled, enjoying the adulation of the guys, but Pete was busy mouthing off. Ranting on about how, when the boss said turtles, he had imagined bloody Turkey at the least, the Caribbean at best, who'd have guessed turtles came to fucking Scotland for their summer holidays. I knew what he meant. When Turner had handed us the assignment I'd thought I would be basking on sun kissed beaches. Scotland has huge beaches, no denying it, but sun kissed? Give me a break; let's just say I made sure my dry suit was packed. I was thinking about crawling into bed when Muriel made an appearance. She walked over to us, the sight of her body doing things to mine which should have been illegal. When I looked round at the others I realised from the fidgeting I wasn't the only one experiencing an autonomic response. She spoke about how we shouldn't go diving the next day, something about upsetting the scalder hunters. We all nodded sagely, as though we knew what she was talking about, but she could have been speaking Cantonese and we'd have agreed. Her voice sounded like the hush of a soft tide running over smooth pebbles.

Up close she looked even more exotic than she had behind the reception desk. Her hair was outlandishly styled like some tribal warrior and an intricate tattoo meandered from behind her left ear, down the side of her neck to disappear, enticingly, below the neckline of her t-shirt. Where did it finish? I wanted to explore. She caught me looking at it and her eyes sparked fierce in the light from the fire. I wanted her to notice me, wanted to stand out from the crowd and said something about not being able to dive in the morning anyway, the forecast suggested there'd be fog when the storm passed. I smiled lazily at her, trying to gauge her interest. There was something lurking there, fire behind the ice. She gave me a measured look and then turned to one of the men standing at the bar, appealing to him to back her up. It was 'Wee Johnny', all of six feet four tall and at least fifty years old. He was booked as our skipper for the dives. He nodded to us amiably enough then confirmed what she wanted to hear – no-one would be going down the next day, the water would be full of sand and weed churned up from the bottom after the blow, we would be diving blind, it was too dangerous. He turned back to his pint, Muriel left, and the bar fell silent. Only the fire, spitting out the salt which had soaked into the wood, made any comment.

The next day I was high on the cliffs by the Mull, watching the ocean for turtles, or to be precise I was watching the sea haar sitting on the ocean for even from the tops by the lighthouse the mist was impenetrable. Occasionally the fog horn would roar its challenge to the monsters of the deep, warning the shipping which probed the North Channel. At the sound a shiver ran down my back. Then I heard the singing, a lilting melody that floated up out of the soft grey. I know mist distorts sound and I couldn't quite catch the language never mind the words, but it seemed obvious, from the tone and the rhythm, that this was a song about longing. It faded, came back at strength and then stopped. I was intrigued. Jogging back down the path I cut right where the cliff had crumbled away and a steep track, filled with scree, led to the beach. I slid more than walked down, the stones clattering around me, and just before I hit the sand was engulfed by the clinging dampness of the fog. I stood for a moment trying to pick up the singing again and was rewarded by the sound of her voice. It was lucky the tide was on the ebb for without thinking I stepped away from the cliff. In less than ten paces I was completely disorientated, wrapped in a cold, silver caress. I walked straight ahead, following the sound.

The mist parted quite suddenly and I could see her, lit by a finger of sunshine. She was sitting on a broad, flat rock about thirty feet out from the shore and in profile the smooth lines of her naked body, the jut of her breasts, were clear. She beckoned me to join her. It took no time to strip off shoes, clothes and wade into the sea, the chill of the water tightening my muscles as it lapped against my belly. I had to swim the last fifteen feet, strong strokes to impress a woman and I saw her smile as though amused.

Muriel's tattoo stretched from her neck, across her shoulders and down the length of her back in an intricate dance of sea creatures; leaping salmon, swirling weed, crabs, orca, skuas, porpoises and shells were all locked into the patterns, their shapes ever melding and changing as the symbols rolled over her skin. They finished in a soft curve a few inches from the base of her spine. Fascinated I ran my hand down its length, feeling her body arch against my fingers, feeling her thrill. She turned to kiss me, wrapped her arms round my neck and slowly fell backwards against the rock, pulling me down to her. The chill left me, blood flared.

At first it was gentle, the exploration of two souls, but then her body became more demanding. I don't know if it was me or the gulls who cried out; don't know how long it was before I fell asleep, spent. Don't know if I woke or if I dreamt I saw, beside me on the rock, the bulk of a leatherback, head raised and green eyes looking out over the waters of Luce Bay. I only know that long hours later the rising sea woke me and dazed I swam back, alone, to the shore. It took me a while to gather my wits and my clothes, longer to struggle into them, looking all the time out to sea. But I saw only a few remnants of the sea haar, burning off beneath the heat of the afternoon sun, and gannets, like white arrows, hunting the herring.

In the Mariner's that night, in the bar again in front of the driftwood fire, Pete asked me where I'd been all afternoon. I just smiled at him, unwilling to share my experience even to claim the twenty five pounds. At dinner I had waited for Muriel to show, hoping she wouldn't regret our lovemaking, wanting the touch of her, the smell of her, but she never appeared. Pete's voice was niggling at me, interrupted my thoughts and I was about to make some excuse about being tired and head off to the sack when I caught sight of Johnny. He was standing at the bar, staring at me. I picked up Pete's empty glass, he nodded and I went for more drinks. The big man was holding an empty pint pot and I offered him a refill. He cocked his head to one side, still looking at me, eyes creased and narrowed by sun and salt. I waved at the barmaid who came over and picked up the glasses. He ordered another Eighty Shillings, I asked for a lager for Pete and my usual Laphroig. As the barmaid busied filling the glasses I asked Johnny about Muriel, if he'd seen her, where she was. I tried to sound casual but even my ears could hear the urgency in the questions. There was a sly look on his face and I got the impression he knew about us. Had he been nearby, in a boat off shore maybe? Up on the cliffs? Would the mist have shrouded us from prying eyes? He took his filled pint glass from the barmaid and raised it in my direction. Our eyes met knowingly across the rim. That was the first time I heard of Gabon, when Johnny told me Muriel was heading that way with her sisters. Said they always left for the equator before the winter set in. He took a mouthful of beer. The barmaid scooped my cash. There was a smile on her lips and as she turned to put the money in the till I glimpsed the edge of a tattoo beneath the collar of her shirt.

We finished the shoot, it was a good documentary, the last time I worked. I'll just finish my rum, swallow the dregs of my pint, go. Where am I off to? There's no moon tonight, it'll be dark on the beach, ideal. I think I'll have a stroll on the strand, think I'll go see if Muriel has touched shore.

Anni Telford was born in Glasgow, lived and worked for thirty plus years as a psychotherapist down in England but now lives in Galloway. She is currently doing an MA in Creative Writing at Edinburgh Napier. Many of her stories and poems are drawn from her love of nature, her interest in Celtic mythology and her experiences of working with the darker side of human nature. As well as writing as an academic she has had short stories and poetry published and is currently working on a trio of psychological thrillers all set in Galloway.

A Small Space

Josie Turner

Eric brought home two full plastic shopping bags. Their handles cut into his fingers.

'I don't need to ask,' said Kath. 'Saturday. Second-hand paperback stall.'

'As a matter of fact,' said Eric, balancing the bags on a slithering glacier of books in the hall, 'I passed a charity shop. They had a sale. Just doing my bit.'

'You're a saint.'

'I thought you'd be pleased. It was for an animal charity.'

'So you've saved the panda. Well done.' She reached out for the nearest book – a ten-year-old travel guide to Venice. 'Where are you putting this lot?'

'I'll find a place for them.'

'Right. Did you get the yoghurts?'

Eric pulled a face. 'Forgot. I can go back out, if you like...'

'I'd rather you didn't.'

Eric and Kath were almost married. They kept meaning to do it, but felt daunted by the paperwork. Eric had moved into Kath's house, twenty years ago, with a single suitcase and a crate of guitar magazines. He would stay at home, looking after the cats, while Kath went out to work. That was the plan. The cats lived long lives in gradually diminishing territory, as books began to fill the rooms. Books muscled along the kitchen counters, and filled the angles of the stairs. Books covered the living room rug and slumped in shoulder high piles in the corners. Books surrounded the doorways after Eric, in a fever of efficiency, constructed shelves above the lintels, and then – exhausted;

amazed at himself – collapsed inert for half a decade. 'Valuable, these,' he would always mutter, contemplating a corner of his collection. 'Rare.'

'Dick Francis is not rare,' replied Kath, although he had not really been speaking to her.

'First edition, that.'

'It is not. You don't know what a first edition is. You don't know what the term means.' These querulous moods would seize her sometimes – after she'd scraped her shin on a vintage Blue Peter annual, or found a favourite handbag crushed beneath a hundredweight of Barbara Vines. Vine, she thought, looking at the paperbacks proliferating across every surface. Good name. Eric's books were growing, spreading, living things; plants thriving in a dusty suburban semi.

On days when Kath stood over his collection with a lighted match, her face crimson with rage, Eric protested that he did read his books. He was always reading. Kath had to concede that this was true. He wasn't one of those collectors who keep everything pristine, behind glass. Eric would read in bed and in the bath and on the lavatory and in the garden. He would read while driving, if he could. He would read while under a general anaesthetic. All he had to do was reach out a hand, wherever he was in the house, and half-a-dozen books would be at his command. He would gorge on words, and then shove the book back into its haphazard berth, tucked up with Harry Potters and showbiz biographies and various histories of the Second World War.

He claimed to have a system; he knew where everything belonged.

'Yes,' said Kath. 'On a bonfire.'

Kath spent a lot of time outside the house – in the office, or the coffee shops of department stores. Her clothes grew shabby and were not replaced, because her wardrobe had been colonised. She kept her jeans and T-shirts folded on a side table on the landing: there was no point buying nice things only to keep them in such conditions. Her diet dwindled to sandwiches and yoghurts; despite eating almost nothing, she put on weight. Eric grew larger and softer, as though he was the blossoming flower of the spreading vine. Unable to find his razor, he grew a beard.

'All my friends tell me I should leave you,' spluttered Kath, on occasion, putting her shoulder to a blocked door. But Eric knew that wasn't true – Kath didn't have any friends. It had become too embarrassing to entertain them. 'You must excuse the mess,' Kath used to say to visitors, in the early days, when Eric was still a novelty. 'He's such a bookworm.' And the visitors would be wide-eyed and diplomatic, even then. But it was impossible, after twenty years, to let anyone inside the house. They wouldn't fit.

'Where are you going?'

'Out.'

Kath could see the broad, shiny seat of Eric's trousers hesitating behind a column of car manuals.

'Out where?'

'...shops.'

The edge of a nylon shopping bag could also be seen behind the column. On especially triumphant days, Eric had been known to fit fifteen hardbacks into this bag.

Kath was on the upstairs landing, and Eric was in the bathroom, which had gradually become the wing of his library devoted to motoring literature. He had unscrewed the door years ago, so the aperture of the doorway was now a jagged gap, perhaps two feet wide, through which each of them had to manoeuvre.

Kath heard a creak, somewhere in the house. A sort of groaning creak. She heard it quite often these days, but she wasn't sure where the sound came from. Perhaps it came from her. She pictured the joists splintering, giving way; the plaster, already cracked, crumbling from the walls. She knew that creatures were tunnelling through the walls, nesting between the pages. The bookworm was burrowing. Her house was alive, although she no longer lived there. You couldn't call this living, she thought.

'I need to brush my teeth,' she said quietly. 'I'm late for work.'

Eric did his best to shuffle past her, but he became wedged by the sink. 'Come through,' he gasped, holding his stomach in.

'I can't!'

'There's still room.'

'There's no room, Eric,' she said in the same quiet voice, with its undertone of creaking, its groan. 'There is no more room.'

A narrow wire shelf unit leaned a few inches into the room. Kath knew the books on that unit must be very heavy; in the kitchen, below the bathroom, the ceiling bulged at that particular spot. Maps, she always thought, eyeing the bulge. Maps of the world. Now the teetering shelves stood between her and Eric, as he stood trapped by the sink, breathing in.

'Come on, old girl,' he said. 'You only need a small space.'

A small space, she thought. That's all I need.

Kath felt peculiar all day, sitting at her desk with un-brushed teeth. She bought a packet of chewing gum at lunchtime. One of the girls had a birthday, and invited everyone for a Friday evening drink. Kath accepted.

'My partner's out,' she explained.

They found a corner booth in a bar, and ordered bottles of wine. They stayed for scampi and chips, and then the cocktails arrived. 'My partner's out,' Kath kept explaining. 'So I can stay as long as I like.'

At midnight, it was agreed that Kath was in no state to find her way home, so she spent the night in Miriam's spare room. Miriam was a spruce divorcee with a ground-floor flat. 'Wow!' said Kath, arriving at midnight. The laminated floors were bare and spotless, and a small illuminated unit contained some china figurines. Four magazines were precisely aligned on a coffee table.

'Excuse the mess,' said Miriam, whipping the magazines away. 'I wasn't expecting a guest.'

In the morning, Kath had a headache.

'You certainly enjoyed yourself,' said Miriam, as she polished the broad leaves of a potted plant on her windowsill. Kath went to replenish her mug of water at the tap, and as she did so she noticed that the plant was artificial. 'Much easier,' nodded Miriam, lifting one of the leaves to show a pale plastic seam beneath.

'I suppose I should be making tracks,' said Kath.

'Will your partner be back home now?'

'Oh no,' said Kath quickly. 'He'll be away for a long time.'

'Got the place to yourself, then? Lucky thing. I'm much happier by myself these days.'

'Yes. I bet you are.'

'Couldn't stand sharing. What's the term? Co-habiting. Urgh!' Miriam shuddered, dropping the plastic leaf.

'It's a nightmare,' sighed Kath. 'Believe me, I could write a book.'

Kath lingered in town. She stopped for a coffee, and then browsed through the fabrics and wallpapers of an interiors shop. Magnolia, she thought, remembering Miriam's immaculate decor.

She decided to walk home, for the fresh air. She put her head down as she passed the library. In her pockets, her hands balled into fists. She was carrying her sandwich lunch in a small plastic bag, and as she walked she recalled recipes from long ago, and her kitchen as it had been twenty years before, with pristine Formica surfaces, and plates neatly arranged in wooden racks. I might make a lasagne, she thought, and open a bottle of wine.

As she approached the cul-de-sac, she felt in her handbag for her keys, and her 'phone.

On the doorstep, she took a deep breath. She closed her eyes. 'Hel-lo,' she called, stepping inside. She wriggled around a mound of Penguin Classics. She placed her keys on a copy of *Wolf Hall*. 'I'm home!'

Silence.

Everything smelled the same – musty, gluey. Not unpleasant. She took off her coat, wondering where Miriam had found her plastic plant. She imagined herself swinging an axe, cutting back a choking vine.

She began to walk upstairs, keeping her 'phone in her hand. At the top of the stairs, she could see that the gap in the bathroom doorway was more jagged than usual, its splay of shadows more complex. The wire shelf unit was lying at an angle, reflecting light in all directions. An atlas had tumbled out of the room and lay open, with the green and brown continents resting upon ideal blue oceans.

Books were his whole world, she thought. I might mention that during the service.

There has been a terrible accident, she thought. That's what I'll say.
She began to dial the appropriate number.

Josie Turner lives in Hertfordshire, and her fiction and poetry have appeared
in publications including *The North, Fractured West, Magma, Mslexia* and *The
Interpreter's House.*
In 2013 her story *Jewels* won third prize in the *Mslexia* short story competition,
and her poem *Rations* won first prize in the Welsh Poetry Competition.
A short story, *The Independent,* is forthcoming as an audio download from
GKBC; *Clinging On* will be published as an audio download from The Casket
of Fictional Delights in August, and *Managing* will appear in *The Frogmore
Papers* in September.

Bertrand

Gerry Cameron

She was in the kitchen making a *petit café noir* with the little espresso machine. She took delight in the ballet of it, turning the handle of the coffee reservoir to release it, flicking forward the plastic attachment with her thumb and using it to hold in the pierced insert whilst she knocked it sharply on the edge of the little white bowl and dislodged the clump of wet coffee grounds in one satisfying move. Then she used the black scoop a couple of times to fill it again with the dark bitter powder she had come to love, tamping it down gently, not too hard, with the back of the scoop then ran it over the edges so that the extra powder fell into the dark red earthenware jar from whence it came. As she reattached the reservoir to the machine, she allowed herself a thought of Bertrand and the day they found the machine at the *Vide Grenier* for 5 Euros (when a new one would have cost 50) and how he had sat all afternoon when they came back with all their loot from the stalls of people selling their household junk and painstakingly used her needle to re-pierce the little reservoir, which was silted up with *calque* from the hard water.

She smiled when she thought of his dark hair falling over his face in concentration, and how later they had stood the machine on the green painted work surface he had made only a month previously for the tiny kitchen and watched with his arm around her shoulder as the machine gurgled its way to fill up the cups that were too large for it really. He'd turned and said with delight, "The things people throw away!" His face was suddenly a boy's.

They had learned its intricacies slowly, this little machine, how to fill without covering the kitchen in coffee, how to use the right amount of pressure to tamp it down, how to judge the result with the froth on top. It was important to do it beautifully, he said.

"*Bertrand...*" she thought – then stopped herself.

The *café* was ready in its little cup with pink rosebuds and she took it into the garden, sitting at the old table and the slatted chair, angled so that she could choose her view, garden or house, as was her delight on these summer mornings. She loved her tall thin house, loved to look at the shutters thrown back against the wall, claret splashes of colour around the back door and the kitchen window. He hadn't finished painting the shutters on the upper two floors, the bedrooms and the *grenier*, which was just shutter and no window beneath, for the house to breath, he'd said she planned to do it in September, when the days were mostly dry, but not so hot. She hoped the paint would last – they'd brought it from England.

They had bought the house for nothing, it seemed, just a little old house in a dilapidated French village, for sale like half the houses around. For them, though, it had been a parcel of gifts, newly discovered each day. The old oak beams in the walls, hidden behind the hideous wallpaper, the ancient tiles of terracotta beneath the rotting linoleum. They could never get them clean enough, but they couldn't bear to cover them up again. And the garden, beneath the waist high weeds, they had discovered simple beds raised in brick, that Bertrand had said was the produce garden. Around the edges were bushes of *hortensia* and giant spikes of rose *tremeins* whose English names she had forgotten. She had admired her neighbour's *wisteria* and together they'd coached some over the fence, so that they could share it. Bertrand again. Left to herself, she would never have spoken to old Mme LaPierre, her hair dyed black, her eyebrows plucked then reapplied thickly with the inaccurate hand that had also put bright orange lipstick onto her thin, mean mouth.

But Bertrand was immune to her baleful stare, the way she ignored them when she came to water her garden. His ringing "*Bonjour Madame!*" had eventually granted him a "*-sieur*" that they could just hear, but he had leant over the wisteria and sought her advice in his very bad French. "*Qu'est-ce que c'est que ça?*" he'd ask, pointing at plants they had uncovered.

Eventually, she began to unbend, for who could resist Bertrand? His intense eyes in the dark handsome face, the way they fell on you and you alone, his enthusiastic interest in everything. The feeling that when you stood in his wake you stood next to life.

Eventually, they sat in her tiny kitchen one day with her *maman*, a frail lady as merry as she was not, each of them clutching a tumbler full of Armagnac and Madame asked about his name, "*C'est Francais, non?*"

"*Ma mere est francaise*," he explained, in the wrong tense. Why didn't she teach you the language, asked madam, reasonably? But he explained that she had died, and that he had always wanted to be here in France, to understand her. Madame nodded and drunk the Armangnac with valiant rapidity.

Never would I have dared this adventure without Bertrand, she thought, platting her hair into a fawn rope over one shoulder. Did he need me?

She thought of the nest of cushions on top of a plastic dust sheet that they had slept in those first days, how they looked in each other's grinning faces and said, "We're in France, *in our house*, can you believe it?" like children who had gone truant. Of course he did, they shared it, like they did the last stale briochette after they spent too much money on paint. She thought how the cushions had scattered as they made giggling, adolescent love.

The bed had arrived along with the instigation of French Fridays (talking in English forbidden) and they thought it lent them a sliver of sophistication, "*Je t'aime*," he'd said and she'd melted into his arms between the soft sheets. "*Mon amour!*" he'd whispered into her hair, but it made her giggle and roll away, helpless to stop. His face froze a little before he caught it, "*Mon Coeur*," he added, with jumping eyebrows and made her shriek.

"*Mon petite chou!*" she'd managed, and he had almost broken their rules, "Wha...Quoi?" She had gulped, "It's what Mme LaPierre says to her cat..." He had caught her up in his arms, roaring, almost falling out of their lovely new bed. Bertrand, her very own Pepi le Pew, the amorous French skunk of cartoons.

Now she was going through her yoga postures, simple stretches, but as she smiled and thought his name, she let him go, aware that there was a well of loss she could visit if she wished and she chose not to.

Bertrand had taught her, as well as many other things, that grief was selfish. It was always about what *you* have lost, not for the other, and as such it may be inevitable, but not encouraged. Not productive. The art of life, said Bertrand, was not to concentrate on what was missing but what was there. And right now, there was so much here – the warmth of the day arising and a warm breeze playing on skin as she felt the blood pulse through her muscles performing the ancient moves. She looked at her feet with attention as she brought her nose as close as possible to the ground, enjoying their splayed solidity on the dry grey ground. Quite beautiful, she thought, but it wasn't a thought really, it was a feeling, a state of being. Nothing was ugly from these eyes, even the scrunched up cigarette pack that Francois must have dropped last night and that was now glowing Gauloise blue under her table.

Another *petit café* while she cogitated on the garden, then leisurely weeded some waves of *concombres* and *tomates* planted like a children's drawing of the sea, because she loathed straight lines.

Francois would visit his aunt today in the *Maison Retraite* where she now lived (still with her ancient maman) bringing tomatoes from the garden that he now tended for her. But she herself would be there before him, probably, with *bonbons de réglisse* for the *maman* and some *hortensia* flowers for madame. She went most days while getting her bread from the *Boulangerie* in the village, only staying long enough to reassure her about her nephew Francois' care of the garden and to listen to the saga of another inmate of the *Maison*, a lifetime enemy of Madame, and how she had been successfully tortured that day. They combatants seemed to enjoy it.

She thought of her friend Anna who had begged her to come home to England after Bertrand was gone. When Madame had gone into the *Maison Retraite*, she had renewed her call.

"What about when you are that age, what about when you need care, have you thought of that? Come home, how can you live like this?"

For a second she had been afraid. She had entered the Scary Future, which, like the Pointless Past was a country Bertrand and she had vowed to no longer inhabit. So she found a job in a *Laboratoire de Rechercher* two days a week and went forward with her life.

Could they, Bertrand and she, have mastered this *Art de La Vie* in

England? He could, she was sure; could have walked the Lake District or the Yorkshire moors with the rapt attention of a Victorian Romantic: Bertrand, with his long dark hair streaming behind with the tails of his floor length green coat.

For them both, though, it was easier here, the constant nudge of the different, the strange, flooding their senses, keeping them awake. The shape of the houses and the decaying twisted barns of the countryside, the patina of shutters, unpainted for years displaying their history of colour through the ages. The labyrinth of French custom and culture, from the '*petits conseils*' of Madame LaPierre, (red wine poured only halfway in the glass, portions of French bread on the table, not on a side plate, all this indicated with a tut-tut for which they solemnly thanked her), to the inscrutable gradations of intimacy (handshake, two kisses, four kisses and the impossible to understand metamorphoses from being addressed formally as "*vous*" to the more familiar "*tu*").

Francois, in her garden last night for some cognac after working in his aunt's garden, listened to the question she had posed to many, "How does one know when the moment comes to use '*tu*'?"

"It's impossible for you English to know." And then he added casually, "But there is a way for you to be sure in this case." He smiled. "You could sleep with me."

Their eyes met over the brandy glasses in a delicious moment. Then she held out her hand "*Oui, s'il te plait.*"

As she led him inside he said, in a chiding tone, "*Non, non. Pas 'te' maintenant...après!*"

Later, in bed, he told her that his wife had left him for his boss.

"The things some people throw away!" She said in English, touching his cheek. He understood only the look in her eye, but he kissed her all the same.

"*Tu es belle, belle,*" he breathed and she tried not to think of French Fridays, tried not to laugh.

She nudged him home after two o'clock, needing the joy of the empty bed. He left with a slight frown, inhabiting the Future, perhaps, she thought.

"There is only now, *cheri*," she whispered in his ear as she opened the door, spilling the light into the dark night. He turned at the gate of the small garden, and it was near enough for her to see his eyes still asking future questions and to feel for a fleeting second, sorry for him.

The first in her bed after Bertrand. He'd said it would be like this, the natural act of a moment, and nothing to do with him at all. She'd denied it to herself, sure that her heart would break when he was gone. It had contracted, certainly, in desperate spasms of pain that could take her in a moment, but hearts like hers, schooled as she had been, did not break. There was always now if you looked and stayed there, just as they'd told each other.

She had been Bertrand's acolyte – quiet and unsure of herself, a victim of tragedy. It would make no difference to say what tragedy, she now believed. All victims are the same, whether of death or abuse, addictions or poverty, they inhabit the same half light, pulled into a cavernous world like vampires who dare not look into the light.

The antidote to pain is so simple that they can't believe it. But she was lucky, Bertrand found her and showed her the escape route, Bertrand who looked like he was blessed from birth with the sunshine forever on his shoulder, when really he was an escapee too, a convert to the light who therefore must pass on his conversion wherever he could.

She thought that being loved by Bertrand had freed her totally, made her feel beautiful, graceful, intelligent and compassionate to all the world.

She said these things to him in her joy, but he said no, it was the loving that did that, not the being loved. She'd smiled a post-coital smile at him, meaning, 'it's all the same' but he'd pulled away from her to sit cross-legged, naked, on the bed.

"Don't you see the difference?" he'd said seriously. "If it's me who makes you feel this way, I can take it from you, too." She'd looked at him, fear cloying through her feeling of safety, "But if it's you, *loving*, that is the real joy then it is within you all the time, whenever you choose."

"But...do you love me, Bertrand?" said the old, frightened one inside her.

"Of course I do," he said, laughing his laugh and sliding in beside her again, "that's why I feel so fabulous."

She came to study those words later, when he was gone. In her grief, whatever she had promised him, she thought about all his words, and much more.

He'd begun to notice the things after a while, like her going out to the bar with him when she'd rather paint or read or buying what he wanted without expressing her own taste. He said to her one night, quite seriously, "Why do you betray me?"

She was winded, almost broken by the blow and just managed, "*Betray...?*"

"Whenever you betray yourself..." His beautiful eyes were stern, then compassionate, "don't be afraid of yourself, we like different things sometimes, it's just a different drum."

She did try then. She lived as he wanted most of the time, for truth be told she was happy to do what he wanted. But more and more she took the time for her own stop and stare. She felt it meant they had more to talk about, more to offer each other when they came together at last.

But that was when he began to be sick. She noticed it first. He was grey and his energy, usually boundless, began to drop. She urged him to see a doctor, but he wouldn't go. He began, quite quickly, to fade away.

They talked about it of course, like they did about everything. He told her what life would be like without him and she couldn't believe his loving reassurances. As usual, she thought smilingly, he was right. After the pain, the way to live was there, still there. Loving the patchwork of little things that make up your day, the sorts of things most people ignore, waiting for their real life to start: the taste of strawberries, the smile of a stranger, the joy of creating. This last, for her a pre-eminent joy, her house, her clothes and garden part of her handmade life.

Today she was shopping in the city. The enormous red holdall she had made contained the necessities to make her visit to Limoges a day treat: sketchbook and tiny watercolour set to continue her little studies of the architecture and *trompe-l'oiel* paintings which covered the gable walls of the Limoges streets and a novel that she could read at the *Salon de Thé* – bliss.

She found herself looking down instead of up as she walked the city streets, for after the rainy morning the afternoon sun had chased the clouds and now shone on the mica in the paving stones, making a dazzling crystal path of Disney magic dust.

Thus she did not see the man who was using a long pole to pull at the awning over his bar, to dislodge the heavy weight of water. She didn't see water drench her but someone did. As she gasped in shock, there was a loud, bellowing laugh from up the street as she stood there for a second, not hearing the waiter's profuse apologies. She knew that voice, she turned towards it. She threw her hands in the air, joyously, her hair splashing the hovering waiter.

"Bertrand!" she shouted.

"*Mon amour!*" he exclaimed making the same gesture with his arms and laughing still.

"*Mon cheri!*" she said advancing steadily towards him now.

"*Mon petite chou!*" he returned.

"*Ma vie!*" She said ringing her hair out as she was almost upon him.
"*Coeur de mon coeur!*"

They were giggling, laughing, as they reached each other – but by mutual assent they held hands, their bodies at arm's length.

"You've got some new lines!" she said, smiling.

He laughed, "I spent three months just crying and watching Pepi le Pew on the cartoon channel."

Their eyes filled as one, and she cleared hers first, wanting to drink him in, every inch of him, her dearest, darling, Bertrand. His eyes held hers, so full of tenderness as always, and something else: happiness again.

"You're in love," she said. Then she saw her, hovering behind him a distance. Shy and unsure, pretty but doesn't know it. Herself seven years ago, except for the age, which she guessed was her own right now.

"I am." He smiled. "And you?" His eyes quizzed her, but of course he could see.

"Even better than that," she said, "loving."

He smiled his fabulous smile at her then, stopping her heart. She hadn't seen the full wattage of that smile since he had begun to be ill.

He'd had the fear, you see, the fear that kills the love. He who had told her to be herself feared her emergence and found himself afraid of losing, and in that fear he lost himself. He could see it, but neither of them could stop it. He wanted to tie her down; therefore he couldn't be around her.

"Tie me!" She'd cried, in desperation. "If that's what it takes to keep you here, tie me hard."

He wept, just wept with her tight in his arms. That was when they started to talk about his going and in just six weeks, he was gone.

"You mean he bloody left you? After dragging you all that way to France? When you were perfectly happy here?" said Anna, when she tried to tell her, the misery still upon her.

Perfectly happy. She had been happy with Bertrand, sometimes perfectly happy, but never before that. She couldn't explain it to Anna, because to do so would be to describe what happiness is to them, what she knew it could be again, thanks to him. That description might limit Anna's sense of her own contentment. It wasn't her right. She had held the phone, looked out of the window and seen the frost of winter bedeck the bare tree, and knew she would be OK.

Her beautiful Bertrand was here, his eyes full of their love. What a joy to have known him, to see him now.

She saw her look, the other girl, worried by the love so clear between them. She could have spared the girl, but didn't. His new partner was in for a fabulous dance, the dance of her life and it was to be hoped a different drum didn't sever all the hope in her. But if it did, she wanted the girl to remember. She could still look and love, still laugh, after him. That might be important for her, whatever it felt like now.

"Back in France!" she said. "Don't tell me where, not yet."

"No!" he agreed. "Not yet."

A squeeze of the hands and a last goodbye, she turned, her face wet with more than the rainwater but her heart filled with her joy and his plus a yearning sharp enough to make today's freedom sweet.

The sun shone fiercely; soon she would be dry.

Gerry Cameron is primarily a Glaswegian crime writer awaiting publication. She's lived in the Highlands and the Outer Hebrides. The story in this anthology is influenced by her holidays in France and her experience of love. Gerry used to write articles for textile magazines and worked as a teacher. Normally she's funny, but sadly not here.

Being Only

Sarah Evans

It's as we approach the automatic doors that I pause to breathe in deeply. The air is scented with narcissi. And then I say it: 'Not today. But another time, I'd like to visit on my own.'

Kay grinds to a waxwork stop as she looks back at me, her mouth slightly open, eyebrows pulling together. I can feel her puzzlement and hurt.

'On your own?' she repeats, posing it as a question so I'll hear how ludicrous it sounds.

'Yes.'

'But I want to see Mum too.'

'I know.' Of course I know. 'I thought you could see her on your own as well.'

'But why?'

It isn't that I don't know why – I've practised my explanations – but I falter for a fatal moment.

'I don't see the point,' Kay says, her voice labouring under the strain of patience. 'I mean we both want to see her; she wants to see both of us. We know how tired she gets and how she isn't up to long visits. Why would we go on separate days?'

'Or at separate times,' I add. I let my eyes rest amidst the double-headed daffodils and wonder how I would feel if it was Kay saying this to me. I've spent my whole life wondering, at some level, what it is like to be Kay. How it is the same. And how it might be different.

'Don't you ever think it's odd,' I say, 'that we never, ever see Mum on her own. Or Dad. It's always both of us.'

She looks at me as if I've completely lost the plot. 'Why would I think that odd?' she asks. Her eyes glisten, unfamiliar in their antagonism. 'This is Theo talking, isn't it?' She nods slightly as if she's realised something obvious. 'It isn't you, it's him.'

'No.' My denial is a bit too vehement; I happen to think Theo might be right.

We walk side by side in uncharacteristic silence along the antiseptic white corridor. A couple of nurses are heading towards us and I see how they look at us and pause mid-sentence. They glance at each other and then smile back our way. Kay smiles too. She likes this, the ripples of sensation we create, wherever we are, wherever we go. We're special. Celebrity status without having earned it. I used to like it too.

Her smile fades as we reach door 331. We look at each other and briefly we clasp hands, bracing ourselves, bracing each other. Two are stronger than one.

Mum's bed has been jacked up and she's wearing the duckling-yellow dressing gown Kay and I chose because we wanted something that was cheerful. Her skin is like watered down milk; her hair has greyed and thinned. Her lips rise up into a smile and she moves her eyes from one of us to the other. 'Kay,' she says. 'Eve.' Proving that she knows who is who. We go and kiss her, Kay and then me. Her cheek is soft as worn leather and she smells of talcum powder and of something earthier.

We sit on the same side of the bed, Kay and me, so Mum doesn't have to keep turning her head.

'How are you?' We chime the words together.

'Not so bad.' It's what she always says, it's what she'd continue saying no matter how close she was to dying. 'Tell me about you.'

Kay chats about her day at work and I tell her about mine. I remind them about my appointment tomorrow, though not because they will have forgotten. I try – and fail – to think how any of this might be different if Kay weren't here.

Mum smiles and nods, though I can see that it's an effort.

She tells us who else has visited and I feel a stab of envy that my aunty Linda gets to drop by on her own and I do not.

'I was thinking…' I start. I don't want to look at Kay, but for some reason that's precisely what I do. Her look is fierce with knowing exactly what I'm going to say. All our lives we've been masters at second guessing one another. Twin telepathy: I've never believed in it, not literally. But twin intuition is not so different.

I've started and I'm determined to go on.

'I was thinking that maybe tomorrow I'll let Kay visit you on her own,' I say. 'And then the day after it could be just me.' My face has flushed and I can feel sweat dripping down my arms as if I've conjured up a fever just by saying this unnatural thing. 'Or if you felt up to it, I could visit after Kay has gone.'

Kay's look of puzzlement and hurt is back but intensified several fold. Mum looks perplexed and worried as she looks from me to Kay and back again.

'Of course I know you're busy,' she says.

'No, it isn't that. It's...' And explaining it to her is no easier than explaining it to Kay. 'I'd just like to see you on your own.' It sounds feeble.

I feel small and hateful knowing that I'm hurting two people I love. I clench everything up tight to stop myself from snatching the words back.

I need to do this; otherwise one day it will be too late.

Kay and I walk back along the corridor to the sound of our synchronised clip-clopping heels. At the entrance she turns to me and says, 'I have no idea what it is you want to say to Mum that you feel you can't tell me.' Her voice is low and flat and it's worse than if she were angry. 'But if it's what you want, why don't you visit her tomorrow. I'll stay away.' She has her martyr look and usually I would relent. All my life at so many times and in so many ways I have always conceded to her; I have always upheld the sacred rituals of our twinship.

My heart keens and aches as I watch her walk away, her shoulders stooping. 'Kay...' She doesn't stop or turn around, leaving me with the knowledge that I can stop her hurt but I'm choosing not to.

Back home I tell Theo what happened. He puts his muscular arms around me; his breath is damp and warm in my ear as he tells me I'm doing the right thing. It provides no comfort.

Dad rings.

'Is everything alright?' I hear the anxiety in his voice and this compounds my guilt. At a time when I truly want to offer him support I'm simply adding to his worries.

'I'm fine,' I say. And I want to scream and shout and ask why this has to be a big deal.

All evening my ears are on standby, alert to my dormant phone as I wait for Kay to call me, the way she always does. Tonight she doesn't. I ring her and I leave a message on voicemail, 'Hi, Kay. It's me. Talk soon.'

I do not say I'm sorry or I was wrong.

I go to bed and much later I wake up with the feeling that I've not slept at all.

'Must be the excitement,' Theo says. 'Maybe a bit of nerves.' I don't contradict him.

We set off for the hospital – a different one – just the two of us. Theo did not want me to ask Kay. We sit in the waiting area with aquamarine chairs and mint-green walls and the scent of artificial lemons. The other women seem further gone than me, their hands resting protectively on top of their rounded stomachs. The time of my appointment comes and goes and still we wait. Theo holds my hand and continues reading his *Economist*. He squeezes my fingers from time to time.

Finally a nurse calls us in and I lie on a couch, which is covered in rustling blue paper. I loosen and hitch up the clothing round my stomach the way I'm told to, exposing pale flesh. The smear of gel will be cold, the nurse says, and she's right. I shiver.

On the screen the black and white image is of a coiled seahorse, blurry and only partially formed. The heartbeat is strong, the nurse says. The single heartbeat. Tears flood my eyes and the nurse hands me a tissue and tells me there, there, lots of women get emotional.

Theo tells her how my mother is ill at the moment and I've been under a lot of strain. He does not tell her how two months ago he spoke quietly and said that if we were to go ahead and have our unplanned baby, if we were to think of getting married and making our relationship work, then some things would have to change.

And I don't tell either of them the reason I am crying. The sea creature looks so lonely. There is only a single heartbeat, when I always imagined there would be two.

Afterwards I go to work and email Kay to say the scan was fine. The day passes slowly; she does not reply. At five thirty I get up and leave and my feet follow the now familiar route along the avenue in which the trees are bursting into spring.

The doors glide open to let me through. The nurse who passes me in the corridor does not seem to see me. I follow the signs for heart-care and I feel seasick with dread. You wanted this: a voice is playing a feedback loop in my head. This is what you wanted.

I go into the room where Mum sits propped up amidst a paraphernalia of equipment. Her eyes meet mine; they look over my shoulder in reflex. She tells me how the doctor has said he'd like to keep her in a few days longer for observation. She hopes to be home by the weekend.

'That's fabulous,' I say.

I show her the print out from my scan and she says how they didn't have those in her day and I know she does not see how there is something missing. We talk of nothing in particular. Silence opens out with no Kay to fill the gaps.

Mum looks at me and smiles, though her eyes are worried. 'Have you and Kay argued?' she asks.

'No,' I say. And then, 'Yes. I mean, sort of.' The argument is of my own making. I wait for Mum to tell me how I should go and make it up with Kay, the way she did when we were little. You'll feel better for it, she'd say; she was always right.

I breathe in deeply. The scent of disinfectant mingles with the fragrance from the roses Dad must have brought in earlier, their buds just starting to unfurl. 'It's just...' I've practised my lines but they are still hard; they feel abrupt. So instead I say. 'Do you remember...?'

She smiles in anticipation. Over the weeks that she has been here, we have often played this game, the three of us, clinging to the past, now the future seems uncertain.

'Do you remember our first day at playschool?' I say.

Mum nods and smiles. Of course a mother remembers these things. 'I had such a job persuading you to go.'

'You told us that we'd make friends. We didn't see the point.' We had each other.

'I had to bribe you with promises of Ribena and chocolate biscuits.'

'The thing that I remember about it...' I say. And I start to talk. It isn't my earliest memory, but it is one of the most vivid.

Mum had dressed us in different colours, 'so everyone will know who is who.' Kay and I looked at each other and giggled. We preferred to be dressed the same; we liked playing games of changing names and seeing how easily grown-ups could be fooled.

The church hall seemed vast and cold beyond the chaotic forest of adult legs which clustered in one corner. We clutched hold of each other's hand very tightly. Mum crouched down to be at our level. 'Why don't you go and play,' she said, and gently tried to steer us towards the smear of colourful skirts and jumpers running round in circles amidst bouncing balls and twirling hoops. The two of us stood and stared. We stared. I turned to look at the face that was like looking into a mirror.

Where are they? I don't know which one of us said it first, or perhaps neither of us said it out loud, but both of us were thinking the exact same thing.

Perhaps they're hiding.

Why would they hide?

'You ask.' That would have been me nudging Kay. Kay would have been the one turning to Mum and voicing out loud the thing that puzzled both of us.

'Where are they?' Kay asked, with her clear bright voice.

'Where are who?' Mum said.

'The others.'

Mum frowned slightly. 'I think this is all there are.'

Kay and I looked at one another. Grown-ups could be so slow.

'The others,' I repeated. 'The twins.'

Mum's face changed then, her frown relaxing and her eyes creasing up into a smile.

'Not everyone has a twin,' she said.

Mum smiles as I reach my punchline. 'I remember,' she says.

'It was such a shock.' The realisation that we were different. I remember feeling so deeply sorry for those other children for being only one. And then I say, 'About Kay...'

Mum's look is serious and I worry that I'm tiring her, placing strain on the heart that has already made its weakness known. 'Should I let you rest?' I ask.

'Tell me about you and Kay.'

'It's just... It isn't really about Kay.' Except that everything has always been about Kay. 'It's just I never got to spend time with you on your own. Nor with Dad.' She nods slowly. 'It was always the two of us. Always. All the time.'

She closes her eyes and I wonder if she's in pain, but she says no, she's fine. I cannot begin to describe how strange and alien this feels, to be sitting in a room with my mother and no Kay.

It's not that we have never been alone. But Kay would always be there in the background, there in the next room, just a shout away, just about to burst in at any moment. We have never deliberately been alone.

Kay has always been at my side. Cuddled up with me in the womb. Lying beside me in the double cot, her thumb in my mouth. Playing with me on the playmat. Sitting next to me at school. Holding my hand on every single outing with Mum and Dad. And even as we grew up and went to different colleges and made different friends and started dating boys, she was always there in the ten times a day calls and texts and emails.

The silence in this small gleaming room weighs down uncomfortably.

Mum breaks it. 'You always wanted to do everything together.'

'I know.'

'Both of you were so adamant. It would have felt cruel to insist on splitting you up.'

'I know.' But we were so young.

'I used to feel jealous,' she says. 'Excluded. It never felt that either of you really needed me. Not when you had one another.' It hurts to hear her say that, a sweet bruising hurt. 'Was it wrong?' she asks.

'I don't know.' And I don't. 'I just don't feel I know you.' Because to know a person you have to spend time with them alone.

I think of those other children, and of pitying them. I think of Kay. I think how she defines me and leaves my outline blurred. How she completes me and leaves me only half-formed. We complement each other, making up for each other's weaknesses. And now I have to learn to do things on my own.

To be a wife, I need to be less of a twin. If I'm to learn to be a mother, I need to learn to be a daughter first.

I reach out and take hold of Mum's hand and we sit quietly for a bit, just my mum and me.

Sarah Evans has had dozens of stories published in magazines and competition anthologies. Highlights of her writing career include: appearing in the 2008 *Bridport* anthology and meeting Fay Weldon at the prize-giving; having several stories published by Unthank Books and receiving great feedback from online reviewers; winning a short story competition run by Spoken Ink whose recording of her story now sits alongside work by many well-known writers. She has also had stories published by Bloomsbury, Writers' Forum, Earlyworks Press, Rubery Press and many more. Sarah lives in Welwyn Garden City with her husband and her interests include walking and opera.

Missing

Kriss Nicol

Something's wrong. There's the smell of cigarette smoke and an atmosphere I don't recognize. It's half-past four and Dad's home. They look up as I walk in and I see something in their eyes. It can't be my fault again. Not this time.

'What's the matter?' I ask.

'Nothing pet. Go upstairs and get out of that uniform.'

I can tell she's lying. She didn't even look up when I spoke. Her eyes are red and she's twisted a paper tissue round and round into a point, like she does when she's trying to get grit out of my eye. Maybe that's why her eyes are red; she's got grit in them.

I don't argue. Don't ask for a peanut butter sandwich first. I do as I'm told. Quickly. Michael's my brother. He's five, I'm ten, and I hate him. Michael's door is open and he's inside, playing. Usually I spoil his games but not today.

What have they found out? I rack my brains to think of what I've done but I just feel sick. I make my way into my bedroom. It's tidy, so it can't be that. Anyway, Dad wouldn't come home for that so it must be Serious.

Changing from my school uniform I put on slacks and a blouse, still unable to remember what it is I could have done. Ah well, I'll just have to face the music. It's a strange saying that, 'face the music'. It sounds like it should be a pleasant experience, but it's not. I wish all I had to face was some classical stuff Dad likes, or the Johnny Matthis songs Mam sings along to. I prefer the Top 40 stuff, like The Searchers and Billy J Kramer.

They're both still sitting at the kitchen table, smoking. Which is odd because they've given up. Their faces are tight, but Mam tries to smile when I come into the room. Perhaps they're going to have another baby and don't know how to tell me. Or perhaps we're moving again. I hope not. It's taken me ages to make new friends and I'm sick of changing schools, getting picked on, feeling miserable. Anything but that!

'We've had some bad news...' Dad starts to say but Mam shuts him up with a look.

'It'll be right as rain, you'll see,' Mam interrupts.

'What will?'

No answer. I'm confused. Has this to do with the new baby or moving? And there's another funny saying 'right as rain'. How can rain be right? And if rain's right, what's left, or wrong?

'Your grandma phoned,' Dad continues.

That's even more weird – Gran never phones. She doesn't know how to.

'It must be a mistake,' says Mam. 'Why don't you go upstairs and play with Michael, there's a good lass.'

She still won't look at me. The bottom of my tummy feels like it's got cramps. It's been doing that a lot recently and I feel hot and cold at the same time. I don't want to play with Michael, I want to stay here with her, but I don't want to disobey her right now either, so I go upstairs.

I've done something really bad this time, I just know it. At Easter the vicar was telling us about how your sins find you out and you're punished for them. Jesus suffered to save our souls so we could go to heaven when we die. I'm not sure how it works, but you have to eat the body and drink the blood of Christ to be saved. It sounds stupid to me. Who on earth wants to drink blood? I thought it was illegal, anyway.

Michael's playing with his cars. He has them all lined up on a board Dad made him with roads, bridges, and traffic lights with zebra crossings drawn on. He's got another board in the spare room with train tracks stuck on it. I like the Rington's tea van and Michael's favourite is a lorry tanker. I usually grab the tanker to make him squawk, but I can't be bothered today. I just sit and watch him play.

I need the toilet. The pain in my tummy's getting worse and my headache's come back. I've been getting it off and on all day and I've had one every day for a while now. It comes and goes, but today it's in the back of my eyes and they're hot. As I go along the landing to the bathroom I feel dizzy and can't see properly. I grab the banister because there are funny little squiggles in the shape of a 'c' in the centre of my vision. The 'c' gets wider as I sit on the toilet and the smell of disinfectant makes me feel worse. Maybe if I lie down it'll go away. I feel awful. My tummy feels heavy and I want to curl up and cuddle it, but I feel sick if I move. My eyeballs don't hurt so much if I close my eyes but I feel the pain in my tummy more. Eventually I make it to my room and lie down.

The 'c' has moved outwards now. It's around the edges of my vision so I can see now, but the headache's getting worse. I'll just lie still and close my eyes till I feel better. I mustn't have wiped myself properly because my knickers feel a bit wet. That's all I need. But I can't get up yet. I'll change them later.

What time is it? I must have dozed off for a bit. I feel groggy – that's a word I like. I came across it in a dictionary and fell in love with it, along with 'guffaw', 'cinch' and 'apoplectic'. It's the sounds of words I love best, before you know what they mean. I like to speak them out loud, roll them around my mouth and taste them before I look the meanings up. I often read dictionaries. You can go on a treasure hunt with them, following words, one word leading to another. Cheryl Wilson and I look for all the dirty words the boys call us but some of them aren't even in. Last week we were learning about penal colonies in RE and Cheryl mis-spelt it and wrote 'penile colonies' instead, which was dead funny but no-one else seemed to see the joke.

I listen for sounds downstairs to tell me what's happening but it's quiet apart from the TV, which is on low. My headache isn't as bad but my tummy's not so good. My knickers still feel damp so I'll have to get up and change them. I'll hide them till I can wash them as I don't want Mam thinking I'm a baby. I remember her face each morning when I used to wet the bed and don't want to go through that again; she's disappointed enough in me already. She gets that look on her face whenever she goes to a parents' evening, or when she finds out about something I've done. Sometimes it's not even me, like the time Jimmy Green put the tadpoles down the girls' toilet, or when Mandy Powell dropped a stink bomb in geography, but I always get the blame.

My God! I'm bleeding! 'Mam! Mam!'

She comes running to the bottom of the stairs. 'What's wrong?'

I try to tell her but I can't stop crying. I'm trying not to panic but I can't help it. She runs up the stairs followed by Dad and Michael. 'Not them, Mam, just you,' I plead. I feel ashamed for some reason.

Mam opens the door and comes in. Dark red clots are clearly visible on my pants and the water in the toilet's red.

'Oh, my sweetheart. What a time for this to happen.'

'For what to happen?'

'Remember I told you about when you turn into a woman?'

'You didn't say anything about blood. Just that my body would change and I'd be able to have babies. I don't want babies,' I sob. 'I want to go to school – we're having a trip to the theatre next week.'

'You're not having a baby. Look, we need to talk but tonight's not the right time. You're fine, nothing's wrong with you, it's perfectly normal. I'm sorry I didn't tell you but things seem to have crept up on us unexpectedly. I was nearly fifteen when mine started.' She puts her arms around me just as the phone rings and I feel her go stiff.

Dad bounds downstairs and the ringing stops. Mam holds her breath. I can hear her heart pounding in my ear, which is resting against her chest. She smells of the little lavender bags she puts in drawers or on hangers to make our clothes smell nice. That smell always makes me feel safe when she comes in during the night to chase the nightmares away. She used to put a nightlight beside my bed because I was terrified of the creatures that roamed my dreams but the shadows that danced on the bedroom walls in the flickering light were just as bad. I snuggle closer.

I hear Dad downstairs on the phone; not what he says but his voice, which is soft, low and dangerous. She exhales and it seems as if life has left her body. She looks down at me as if she's never seen me before and gently wipes the tears from my face. Her eyes soften before brimming with tears that spill over onto her cheeks.

'Come on, let's get you cleaned up,' She says as she passes me lots of toilet paper. 'I'm just going to get something.'

Dad's outside the door again and she falls into him. He folds her up in his arms and they cry into each other's hair. Michael's looking confused and tearful but I don't see any more as I kick the door closed. Mam returns in a couple of minutes with a facecloth, my pyjamas, an elastic belt and a long white pad of cotton wool with loops. I wash myself and she shows me how to use the belt and attach the pad so it fits under me, like a suspension bridge. It feels big and bulky but I don't complain.

'Off to bed now. We've to go to grandma's tomorrow so try to get some sleep. We'll talk about this in the morning.'

'Why are we going to grandma's?' My voice wobbles because I'm afraid. This isn't normal at all, especially on a school day.

'Brian's missing. He didn't come home from school.'

I laugh with relief. So it's Brian who's in trouble, not me. Brian's my cousin and, according to my gran, a right little tearaway, just like me. 'He'll just be at someone's house,' I scoff. 'Remember when I forgot the time and...'

'No, sweetheart,' Dad interrupts, 'it's more serious than that. Someone saw him playing down by the pier. They think he might have fallen in. The coastguard has just called off the search. They'll try again in the morning.'

I'm stunned. Mam kisses me goodnight and I go to bed. I lie on my back, hands across my chest, and feel as if I'm in a coffin, listening to the sounds of the house; the clock in the hall, the pipes gurgling and knocking. Mam and Dad go downstairs and I hear the kitchen door closing. Someone fills the kettle and I hear the muffled sounds of crying. It's like the whole house is heaving and sighing, mourning for things lost. I feel blood ooze from me and search for a word to describe how I feel. I can't find one.

Kriss Nichol is a retired teacher with an MA in Creative Writing who moved to SW Scotland over ten years ago to concentrate on her writing. She writes poetry and fictional prose and has had numerous poems and some short stories published in various small press magazines and anthologies. Her first novel is available on Amazon, a second is finding a publisher and a third is a work in progress.